Rebecca's Dream

Brides of Cedar Falls, Book #8

Jo Grafford, writing as Jovie Grace

SECOND EDITION March 2025: This book was originally part of the Brides of Pelican Rapids Series. It has since been rewritten and expanded to be part the **Brides of Cedar Falls Series** — swoony historical romance full of faith, hope, love, and cowboys!

ISBN: 978-1-63907-084-8

Acknowledgments

Many thanks to my editor and friend, Cathleen Weaver, and Karen Edwards for working their magic on this story. I'm also enormously grateful to my beta reader, Mahasani. Another big shout-out goes to all the Cuppa Jo Readers out there for reading and loving my books!

For more about my books —>

Follow on Bookbub
https://www.bookbub.com/authors/jovie-grace

Follow on Amazon
https://www.amazon.com/author/joviegrace

Read FREE Bonus Stories
https://www.JoGrafford.com/bonuscontent

Join Cuppa Jo Readers
https://www.facebook.com/groups/CuppaJoReaders

Chapter 1: Leaving Town
Rebecca

August, 1871

Rebecca Copeland shuddered as she took her final walk through the stately old mansion that had been her home for the past twenty years. She was surrounded by bittersweet memories of her lost loved ones. It felt like walking among ghosts. The only sound was the swish of her gown as she moved wordlessly through the parlor, library, and dining room.

The curtains were pulled closed, and the furniture was covered with dust cloths. Tomorrow the bank would proceed with their foreclosure. She would be hundreds of miles away by then.

She could still picture the way her father used to lounge with one elbow resting on the stone mantle between the floor-to-ceiling bookshelves in the drawing room. Lincoln Copeland, better known as Linc to his fellow plantation owners on the outskirts of Atlanta, had never grown weary of watching his beloved late wife, Clara, with her blonde head bent over her embroidery projects. Her signature hydrangea and magnolia blooms were stitched on nearly every piece of linen inside their only daughter's hope chest. It was locked and awaiting transport on the front veranda.

Rebecca pressed a fist to her mouth to muffle a sob as she stared out the back picture window at the vast acres of farmland and pastures. Her two brothers, one a year younger than her and the other two years older than her, had been so full of restless energy and unfulfilled dreams as they dashed in and out of the barns before their many hunting expeditions. Sadly, their dreams would forever remain unfulfilled. The war had seen to that. Both Jonathan and Michael were now resting in the Marietta National Cemetery, alongside her father and countless friends.

"Come, dearest. It's time to go," Hope Thompson announced softly. She was standing beneath the arched entryway to the library. Her low, melodic alto was infused with a world of understanding and sympathy. She was no stranger to suffering herself as, one by one, her parents, siblings, aunts, uncles, and cousins had made their way north during the war on the Underground Railroad. Rebecca's mother had been instrumental in securing their passage, right up until a stray Union bullet had put an end to her faithful dedication to the cause.

Refusing to leave her best friend to face so many tragedies alone, Hope had lingered behind the rest of her family. And lingered some more, until Rebecca could no longer imagine life without Hope, especially during the next adventure they were about to embark on.

"I'm ready." She blinked rapidly to hold back her tears. There was nothing left for either of them in their devastated and impoverished home state. The foreclosure of her childhood home would serve as the final nail in the coffin of the Copeland dynasty. Her attorney had promised to handle it in her absence at no additional charge. It was his parting gift to her, a tribute to her dearly departed family.

She was an orphan now, and Hope was as good as one herself; but they had each other and her small savings that she intended to stretch as far as it would go. It would be enough. It *had* to be enough for the long journey west. Neither of them had anyone else to turn to. The few neighbors still standing after the war were barely making ends meet.

It had felt like divine intervention a month ago when Rebecca had read the advertisement for a teaching position in Cedar Falls, Texas — a small country town she prayed would turn out to be as cozy and welcoming as they'd made it sound in the newspaper. It was a huge point in their favor that they'd been willing to hire Hope as her teaching assistant. Rebecca had insisted on making it a condition of her contract. Though Hope and her family had once served as slaves on a plantation across town, Rebecca had stressed in her application that she was like family. She'd enjoyed the same private tutoring sessions and received the same education as herself. It would be a shame if they changed their minds after laying eyes on her dark skin, but they would cross that bridge when they came to it.

They were only being provisionally hired — providing backfill for the teacher who normally served in that role. All Rebecca knew about her was that she was on a leave of absence.

The mayor of Cedar Falls, a man by the name of Reggie North, had traded a series of letters with Rebecca over the past few months. She patted the stack of letters in the pocket of her travel gown — black satin for mourning. She and Hope planned to read through the letters again the moment the train left the station. They would do it as many

times as it took to ensure they were prepared for their new
duties.

"You have them?" Hope's expressive brown eyes
glowed with anticipation. Her thick, ebony hair was
pulled back in a snug chignon to contain her natural riot
of curls. It was a style Rebecca thought of as her regal
look.

"I have them." She swallowed a lump of sadness at the
unlikelihood she would ever again step foot in her childhood home. She attempted to paste on a smile, but she
wasn't sure she succeeded.

Hope was wearing a gown Rebecca had insisted she
borrow for the journey. She wanted the two of them to face
the world together as the equals they were — not wanting
everyone they encountered to mistake Hope for her servant.
She couldn't have been more pleased with Hope's
appearance.

Hope was stunning to begin with, with high cheekbones
and lush, full lips. The lavender silk gown she had on
merely served to accentuate her complexion and the exotic
slant of her eyes. Her borrowed jacket boasted a sheer lacy
overlay, and a row of embroidered lavender blooms ran from
her throat to her trim waistline.

"Are you having second thoughts about me wearing
this?" Hope ran her hands uncertainly down the full skirt of
her gown. "It's not too late to change your mind. It wouldn't
take long to unpack my calico dress and make it
presentable."

"I'm not having seconds thoughts." *Not about that, at
any rate.* Rebecca's smile wobbled. She was filled with
misgivings about nearly everything else. "If I look out of
sorts, it's only because I'm dreading leaving all of this
behind." She fluttered her hands in agitation at the library.

4

"This place is full of so many memories." Her voice trembled.

"It is for me, too." Hope's voice was thick with emotion. "But the best ones will remain here. Forever and always." She pressed a hand over her heart.

Rebecca blinked back more tears. "You always know what to say to lift my spirits." She was grateful all over again that she wouldn't have to make the long journey west by herself.

"We've had years of practice jawing to each other." Hope waved a finger playfully between them. "Which brings us back to my original question. Are you sure about my outfit?"

"Very sure." Rebecca reached out to adjust the dust cloth covering the pianoforte, the one item of furniture she was going to miss above all the others. "We agreed that outfitting you like a lady of means would be the best and safest way to travel." She wanted Hope to be treated with the dignity and respect she deserved, and what she was wearing would help make that happen.

"Some folks might think I'm putting on airs." Hope flicked idly at one of the ruffles on her skirt.

"Let them." Rebecca tilted her heart-shaped face to study her friend through critical eyes, trying to see her as the other passengers on the train would see her. "My advice is to keep your chin up and shoulders back, no matter who we encounter."

Hope rolled her eyes. "That's easy for you to say, my dear Mistress of the Manor."

"I'm no longer that person," Rebecca reminded with a tight smile. "From now on, I'm mistress of nothing more than a pile of travel bags and trunks. *The same as you.* Granted it was an impressive pile, since it contained all of their earthly possessions. She smoothed a hand over the white-blonde hair she'd twisted up, wondering how long she'd make it before all the pins gave her a headache. She'd probably end up throwing propriety to the wind and letting her hair down by nightfall.

"Not true. You'll soon be presiding over the schoolhouse at Cedar Falls." Hope glided with her into the elegant entry foyer.

"Co-presiding," Rebecca reminded. "For as long as we're needed." The only downside to the positions they were accepting was their temporary status. Miss Charlotte Carmichael, who normally taught at the one-room school-house in Cedar Falls, had been summoned to her sick father's bedside. The length of her leave of absence was unknown, which was why the board had been forced to advertise for a temporary replacement. Rebecca and Hope would be searching for employment again as soon as Miss Carmichael returned to duty.

After spending the first twenty years of her life in pampered luxury, it was a daunting prospect for Rebecca to be stepping into a job full of so many unknowns. But desperation had propelled her to accept the first offer that came along. Even a temporary job was better than no job at all.

"I'm confident the Lord will provide our next offer of employment, just like He provided this one." Hope glanced over her shoulder to ensure that Rebecca was following her. "It's past time for us to skedaddle to the train station." Her voice grew softer as she added, "The train won't wait for us if we're late."

It was a gentle reminder that nobody would wait on the last surviving Copeland any longer. Rebecca's family name had become one that was spoken in hushed tones out of pure pity. It no longer opened doors or made folks sigh with envy like it once had.

She tamped down on a burst of genuine terror as she mentally reviewed her final checklist for the journey ahead. Most importantly, every member of her family's staff had been dismissed with glowing letters of recommendation. She'd personally seen to it, penning them with her own hand. Everyone, except for the cook who'd decided to retire, had already secured new positions. Rebecca's life as a southern belle was over. Her life as a member of the working class was about to begin.

"Please, Lord." She sent up a silent plea from the deepest, most anxious depths of her heart. "Be with us on our journey." Then she followed Hope outside to the veranda and locked the door behind them.

Ezekiel, her former driver, was waiting for them in a sleek black carriage. He was grinning widely. "Good mornin', Miss Rebecca. Mornin', Miss Hope." He tipped his cap at them. Gone was his former navy suit that her father had given him. In its place was a black and white livery uniform, bearing the faded Harrington family crest. The Harringtons were struggling to eke out a profit on one of the neighboring plantations. Rebecca hoped they succeeded.

"Good morning, Ezekiel! How can I ever thank you?" As Rebecca stepped further into the sunlight, it dawned on her that she'd entirely forgotten to arrange transportation for them. In the past, it hadn't been necessary since her family had always kept a driver on staff. Fortunately for her, Hope hadn't forgotten about her newly impoverished state. Rebecca knew without asking that this was her doing.

"It was no trouble, ma'am." Ezekiel doffed his work cap at them again, grinning widely as he leaped down from the driver's seat. "Mr. Harrington said he could spare me fer an hour or so to git yer things to the depot." He tossed their bags and trunks on a rack above the carriage as if they weighed no more than twigs.

"Please give him my kindest regards and heartfelt thanks." Rebecca hurried forward to grab the handles of her nearest travel bag.

"Allow me, Miss Rebecca." Ezekiel blasted her with one of his most ferocious scowls. "Save yer strength for the journey." He winked in Hope's direction, confirming something Rebecca had always suspected. He was sweet on her friend, making a big show of shooing away her assistance. "You won't be messin' up that dress on my watch." His dark, admiring gaze returned again and again to Hope's borrowed gown.

Rebecca sent Hope a questioning look, praying she wasn't single-handedly tearing apart two lovebirds. However, Hope shook her head when Ezekiel's back was turned, looking suspiciously close to chuckling. Rebecca's shoulders relaxed at the realization it was one fear she could cross off her list.

Ezekiel kept them entertained all the way to the train station with stories about his younger brothers' antics. Oh, how Rebecca was going to miss him and his precious, hardworking family!

When they arrived at the train platform, he again waved away their attempts to help unload their belongings. "It may be the last thing I ever git to do fer you, Miss Rebecca." He inclined his head respectfully at her.

She was too choked with tears to give him more than a damp nod. She wanted to beg him to write to her and Hope, but she sorely doubted he could read or write. Instead, she watched him unload their bags and trunks and place them in the care of a porter. When he returned to say his final goodbyes to them, she discovered she'd lost her power of speech altogether. However, words weren't necessary. With her heart in her eyes, she held out her arms to him.

Ezekiel's wide, friendly features registered a mix of surprise and gratitude. He gave her the gentlest of embraces that was edged with reverence. "God be with you, Miss Rebecca," he muttered gruffly.

She tearfully smiled her thanks to him. *God be with you and your family, as well.*

"He's a good man," Hope announced softly as they took their seats in the train car they would be traveling in. "I'm going to miss him terribly, along with his rapscallion brothers."

"They don't come any finer than Ezekiel," Rebecca agreed, giving her friend another searching look. "Please assure me again that I didn't make a horrible mistake by taking you away from him." Unless their financial circumstances took a drastic turn for the better, she and Hope wouldn't be able to spare the funds for another set of train tickets anytime soon.

Hope shook her head. "I adore him and his brothers to pieces, but that is all. We grew closer after my family moved north." She'd been forced to bid a hasty farewell to her parents and siblings, all of whom were now gainfully employed in a Philadelphia farming community.

"My heart says Ezekiel has considered the possibility of asking you to be more to him," Rebecca pressed quietly. "He would've already done so if you'd given him the least bit of encouragement."

"As much as I wish to deny it, I cannot." Hope's voice grew sorrowful. "His feelings for me have given me all the more reason to leave. He may not be book smart, but he understands that the miles between us will make anything beyond friendship impossible."

Her answer underscored just how much she'd given up to remain by Rebecca's side. "If you had found it in your heart to return his feelings," Rebecca said carefully, "please know that I would've never come between the two of you."

Hope's eyes widened in mock dismay. "You would've left me behind, eh?"

"Or not applied for the teaching position at all." Rebecca shook her head in bemusement.

Hope looked displeased with her answer. "What would you have done without a job?"

"Pick cotton, I suppose." Though it was a serious question, Rebecca had no better answer. "While praying for a miracle." She'd never had to depend on the Lord to supply her most basic needs, but other people did it all the time. Surely, she would get used to the feeling.

Hope's frown was replaced with an expression of pure astonishment. "Most women in your position would be hunting for a husband."

Rebecca turned to look out the window and found Ezekiel standing on the platform, waving with energy at them. She waved back. "I'm afraid my husband-hunting days were over before they began." Her battle with scarlet fever during her teen years had put a brutal end to that particular dream. According to her doctor, the fever had rendered her unlikely to ever bear children.

"Nonsense," Hope snapped, leaning around her to wave. At the sight of her, Ezekiel's dark features brightened considerably. "We'll begin your hunt anew in Texas."

Rebecca leaned back in her seat to give Hope more room to wave. "I refuse to sentence anyone else to the burden I must carry." God seemed to have other plans in store for her — plans that would allow her to nurture untold numbers of children in the schoolroom.

"It might be best to leave those kinds of details up to the Lord." Hope's tone was mildly censuring. "He's never steered us wrong." She didn't sound convinced that Rebecca was destined for spinsterhood.

"You have no idea how much I want to believe you." Rebecca gazed into the distance. "But we're both old enough to know we don't always get what we want. I prefer to remain practical."

Her penchant for practicality was the sole reason she'd selected a bench for them at the farthest end of the train car. So far, no one else had chosen to sit across from them. With Hope's attention so focused on Ezekiel, she likely hadn't yet noticed all the curious and hard-eyed stares aimed in their direction.

"Donning bright feathers does not a peacock make," one woman muttered to her travel companion as they turned away from the end of the car and bustled back up the aisle.

Rebecca's heart sank, knowing she was referring to Hope's borrowed gown.

"See? I should've worn my old calico," Hope hissed. Her shoulders slumped in discouragement. "I rightly figured that folks would think I'm overstepping my place."

"Your place is with me," Rebecca hissed back, hating that a horrid fellow passenger had gone to such lengths to make Hope miserable. She reached for the packet of letters in her pocket. "We're family, which is what I'll tell anyone who asks." If it weren't for Hope, she'd be alone in the world. Even worse, she'd be traveling hundreds of miles unaccompanied — while in mourning, no less.

From the corner of her eye, she gauged the worried wrinkle on her friend's forehead and decided it was high time for a distraction. She unfolded the first letter and smoothed it open. It was from Mayor Reggie North.

"I feel the same way." Though Hope continued to smile at Ezekiel, her smile had grown forced. "I don't know what I would do without you."

You'd be living in the north with your blood relatives, that's what! Shivering, Rebecca forced the thought away. "Are you ready to re-read the first of many letters that changed our lives?"

The train gave a few sharp hoots of warning about their pending departure, prompting Ezekiel to wave his final wave and trot off the platform.

Hope watched him until he disappeared into the crowd thronging the base of the platform. Then she settled back in the seat, leaning companionably toward Rebecca. "I can't think of anything I'd rather do."

Rebecca promptly began to read.

Dear Miss Copeland:

Congratulations on earning your teaching certificate. I'm delighted you're willing to make Cedar Falls School your first station. It isn't easy finding qualified candidates for such a rural area. You're the first one, in fact, who's met every condition we were hoping for.

Our current teacher has been summoned out of state to her father's bedside. Since no one knows how long she will be absent or when she will return, the school board has voted to hire a temporary replacement. I pray you will accept the generous terms of our offer and travel to Cedar Falls with haste. Not only are the students in urgent need of your assistance, I will selfishly admit that the prolonged absence of a certified teacher reflects poorly on me as a mayor.

Rebecca could almost hear the rueful chuckle he'd surely given while writing the last sentence. "He sounds like he has a sense of humor."

"Indeed, he does." Hope nodded. "Little does he know we started packing the same afternoon we received this letter."

"I'll never forget the day." The mayor's job offer had come like a ray of light during one of their darkest hours. Rebecca dipped her head over the letter and continued reading.

In anticipation of our regular teacher's return, I put a bug in the ears of several local business owners, who have assured me there are plenty of employment opportunities around town. I have it on good account that we can always use another seamstress, waitress, or farm hand.

None of the positions he mentioned were glorious, but they would help keep food on the table.

"That's assuming any of them will be as willing as the mayor to hire a black woman." Hope cast a baleful glance around them.

Rebecca followed her gaze and was relieved to discover they were no longer attracting as much attention as they had when they boarded. She returned her attention to the final lines of Mr. North's letter.

Please don't be alarmed by what I write next, but it's only fair to warn you. One of our oldest board members takes particular delight in playing matchmaker, and she is inquiring if the two of you are betrothed.

Hope gave a breathy chuckle that died when the ticket

master trudged determinedly in their direction. He was a young fellow with slicked-back hair and sharp creases pressed into his navy uniform. "Good morning, ma'am." He addressed Rebecca, ignoring Hope altogether. "Your ticket, please."

"Good morning, sir." She handed both of their tickets to him.

The ticket master frowned at the second ticket for a pregnant moment before taking it. "Ma'am, if you'd like your servant to retire to the back of the train, we have a special car for her kind." He dropped his voice, leaning conspiratorially closer to her. "It'll keep the complaints to a minimum, if you know what I mean."

Her kind, eh? Though his words infuriated her, Rebecca pretended to be surprised. "Dear me, no! Our driver, Ezekiel, is not coming with us today." She made an exaggerated show of glancing in both directions. "I thought he'd already taken off."

The man straightened. "I'm referring to the woman sitting next to you," he intoned with a deadpan look.

Of course, you are, you numbskull! "Ah." She reached for Hope's hand to pat it affectionately. "Miss Thompson is not in my employ. She's my dear friend and travel companion." She gave a dramatic sigh fit for the stage. "I wouldn't have made it this far during my mourning without her faithful companionship."

"Well, I never!" The woman across the aisle from them sent a fuming look at the man accompanying her. He either didn't hear her or pretended not to hear her, remaining ears deep in his newspaper.

Before the ticket master could react, a commotion rose from the entrance to the car. It was accompanied by a few female gasps and a muffled shriek of outrage. Rebecca whirled around and discovered a tall man in a Stetson, denim trousers, and well-worn boots striding up the aisle. As he drew closer, he removed his hat, revealing heavily tanned features framed in wind-tousled blonde locks. He had the look of a man who spent a great deal of time outdoors.

But that wasn't the reason for the commotion.

Rebecca's gaze flitted past him to the man striding a few steps behind him. He was equally tall and outdoorsy looking, but the resemblance stopped there. He was as dark-skinned as Hope.

The woman who'd refused to sit near her earlier gave an indignant squeak. "Two of them in the same car? What's the world coming to?" Her bleats of protest were aimed at no one in particular, and no one bothered answering her.

"Goodness," Hope murmured behind her hand, giving a nervous titter. "This trip just got a lot more interesting."

Rebecca wasn't surprised when the two men claimed the empty bench facing her and Hope. As far as she could tell, it was the only available spot in the car.

The blonde man nodded at her and held out a hand, scanning her with his disconcerting blue gaze. A scar running jaggedly from the corner of his left eye to his earlobe told her he wasn't a man to be trifled with. "Since we're going to be on this train a good while, we might as well introduce ourselves. I'm Hank Abernathy, and this is my business partner, Pete Bishop." Though his accent was similar to Rebecca's, it held a hint of something else. He wasn't originally from the south. She would bet all the money she no longer possessed on it.

She wasn't normally given to nerves or shyness, but placing her hand in his much larger one made her feel self-conscious. Vulnerable, even. It wasn't a feeling she was accustomed to.

"I'm Rebecca Copeland." She shook his hand, then reached over to shake the hand of his associate. "I'm pleased to meet you. This is my friend, Hope Thompson." She turned expectantly to Hope, but not before she caught the slight widening of Mr. Bishop's eyes. He appeared as surprised as the ticket master had been to learn that Hope was not in her employ.

"Pleased to meet you." Hope observed the two men demurely from beneath half-lowered lashes, hesitantly extending her hand.

Rebecca's heart went out to her as the broad-shouldered Mr. Bishop eagerly grasped it. Hope was painfully shy around strangers. Meeting two new gentlemen at the same time must be excruciatingly uncomfortable for her.

"I assure you the pleasure is all ours, ma'am." Mr. Abernathy leaned Hope's way to capture her hand the moment Mr. Bishop let go of it. "You're a far lovelier sight than what we had to endure on our last journey by rail."

The train lurched into movement, making them sway in their seats, as it rolled forward.

His compliment brought a warm blush to Rebecca's cheeks. "Where might your destination be, sir?" Though their train was bound for Texas, Texas was a big state. It was unlikely their paths would converge there.

"Hank," he corrected quickly. "Just call me Hank. Pete and I aren't accustomed to standing on ceremony." He glanced around them, not bothering to hide his disgust at the behavior of their fellow passengers. The train gained speed as it eased away from the station.

The thought of being on a first-name basis with a complete stranger made Rebecca's insides twist with misgivings. It was probably enough to make her oh-so-proper southern mama roll over in her grave.

"We're in the process of relocating our horse breeding business out west," Hank Abernathy continued in a conversational voice, as if he hadn't just finished making the social *faux pas* of the century.

It was an interesting vocation — different from all the farmers and plantation owners Rebecca had grown up around. Her fascination with him and his companion grew. "That's the same direction we're heading, sir...that is, Hank." She ventured a glance at Hope and found her attention shyly fixed on Mr. Bishop. Or Pete, as his business partner clearly preferred to call him.

"I doubt it's the same town. More's the pity." Hank shot her a grin so admiring that it made her toes curl in her travel boots. "We're heading to a place called Cedar Falls. Not big enough to make more than a speck on a map, but we've done our research. It's a peaceful town filled with honest folk. A slice of countryside not still smoking and smoldering from the aftershocks of war." He caught his partner's gaze, and they exchanged a knowing look.

Rebecca's lips parted on a gasp of astonishment. "That's *exactly* where we're heading!" What were the odds? "I've accepted a temporary position to teach school there. Hope will be assisting me." She hastened to fill in the stunned silence that followed her announcement. "Their regular teacher had to take a leave of absence to care for a family member, so we're not sure how long our services will be needed." Or how long they'd be staying afterward. There were too many unknowns at the moment to predict what would come next for them.

"Is that so?" For reasons that made no sense to her, Hank's gaze narrowed in speculation at her. "You haven't, by any chance, been in touch with a woman by the name of Winifred Monroe?"

"No, we haven't." Rebecca had never heard the name of the woman in question. She self-consciously drew back the folds of her skirt that were spilling into the narrow walkway between their benches. "We've been corresponding exclusively with Mayor North. Why do you ask?" Including his name in their conversation made her sound well connected, though nothing could be further from the truth. She'd lost her childhood home to the bank and was currently as poor as a church mouse.

"Idle curiosity." Hank's gaze raked her and Hope's custom-tailored gowns and came to rest on her black leather boots. "I reckon that means you're not the two ladies she's picked out for us to marry."

Chapter 2: The Ungentleman
Rebecca

"Marry you!" Rebecca glanced around them in alarm. If there were any empty seats left on the train, she would've immediately relocated herself and Hope, but there were none available. Her initial impression of the too-handsome-for-his-own-good Mr. Hank Abernathy plummeted. The man sounded demented.

Pete Bishop broke the awkward silence with a chuckle that held a surprisingly empathetic note. He aimed a playful punch at his partner's upper arm. "Aw, Hank! You're frightening the ladies." His bourbon eyes brimmed with humor as they moved between Rebecca and Hope. "He can't help his lack of social graces. He was raised in a barn."

A titter of amusement escaped Hope, but she clapped a hand over her mouth as shyness overcame her once again.

"We both were," Pete confessed a bit shamefacedly. He gestured at Hank. "Former indentured servant." Then he pointed at himself. "Former slave."

Rebecca frowned in confusion at them. Life had taught her not to be overly trusting. "You both sound mighty educated for such humble backgrounds." So did Hope, but it was only because Rebecca's family had made her an honorary Copeland. She was the exception, not the rule.

"Aye, an' we 'ave the mistress of the manor ta thank fer that," Hank drawled, pronouncing the word *manor* with a drawn out last syllable that sounded more like *air*.

"You're Irish," Rebecca declared in an *aha* voice, tickled to discover that her original guess about his lack of southern roots was correct.

He curled his upper lip at her. "You, on the other hand, are as southern as the magnolia blooms on the uppity trees we're leaving behind."

Uppity! Her affronted gasp made Pete scowl. "Easy, brother."

Hank scowled back, indicating he had no interest in toning down his grumbling about the city they were departing. Or its upper echelon, which he'd apparently decided she was part of. He slouched down in his seat, wiggling to get more comfortable. Then he stretched his long legs out in front of him, crowding her leg space.

While she was busy yanking her skirt away from his boots, he propped his Stetson on his head and pulled it over his face, hiding everything but his stubborn chin from view.

"It's a good thing you're not the woman I'm supposed to marry." His words were muffled behind the brim of his hat, "because I'd be tempted to call the whole ceremony off, right here and now." He crossed his arms over his chest. Moments later, his breathing evened into sleep.

All Rebecca could do was stare at him, openmouthed. "I'm not planning on marrying anyone," she finally muttered. "Ever."

Hope's hand curled reassuringly around hers as she summoned the courage to rejoin the conversation. "Neither of us plans to marry."

Mr. Bishop's chagrin was immediately replaced with curiosity and no small amount of concern. "I'm sorry to hear it." His voice grew hushed. "It's a story we've run across all too often across the southeast." He shifted uncomfortably in his seat. "If I had a penny for every young woman who's been abused by her master...ahem, former master." His jaw tightened as fury took over. "I don't understand why the good Lord allows such things. I truly do not."

"Oh, dear!" Hope looked mortified. "Our reasons are most thankfully not anything of the sort! The family who took me in was everything that was kind and generous, may they rest in peace." Her voice took on a note of reverence. "Rebecca's mother gave her very life in service to the Underground Railroad."

Mr. Bishop's shoulders relaxed. "I beg your pardon. I stand corrected." He inclined his head respectfully at her. "Is that why you remained in Atlanta for so long? I can only presume your means of escape perished with her."

Hope stiffened and drew herself upright. "If I'd wished to run from everything I hold dear, you may be assured I would've found a way." She squeezed Rebecca's hand tightly. "But as Ruth stated in the Good Book, where this woman goes, I will go. Until the end of our days, if the Lord allows it."

"Now *that* is a sentiment I can get behind." Pete Bishop's friendly smile returned. He cast an eager glance at his sleeping friend. "The dusty cowboy beside me and I have a similar story, if you'd care to hear it."

Before Hank's stinging barb at her, Rebecca would've begged him to continue his story — anything to divert their attention and make the long journey pass quicker. However, she had no interest in learning more about his crass companion.

Rebecca and Hope's ensuing silence pulled a gusty expulsion of regret from him. "Clearly, Hank and I got off on the wrong foot with you. Perhaps you'd be kind enough to let us apologize and start over?"

"You don't owe us an apology, Mr. Bishop." *Your sleeping friend does, but I won't be holding my breath on his account.* Rebecca kept her head high and her voice prim. Inwardly, she was still seething over Hank Abernathy's crude rejection of her as his potential bride. Not that she had any desire whatsoever to become tethered to the likes of him.

"Hank certainly owes you one." Pete cast another look at his sleeping companion, looking like he wanted to throttle him. "I assure you he didn't mean a word of what he said. He only gets defensive like that when he feels slighted."

"Slighted!" Rebecca spluttered out the word. "Why, we were nothing but kind to him!" How dare he try to pin the blame of their altercation on her! No matter how skilled Hank Abernathy's command of the English language was as an immigrant, he was still plagued with ill manners — something a person couldn't blame on their culture or background. As far as she was concerned, being kind to others was a choice, and he'd made the wrong choice.

Pete raised his hands defensively. "Indeed, you were all that was kind, ma'am. It was your response to his mention of marriage that raised his hackles. After what happened to him back in Atlanta..." He lowered his voice and cast a furtive glance at his friend, as if trying to gauge if he was sleeping. "Simply put, a certain high-society lass broke his heart, and he has yet to recover from it."

From his heartbreak or something else? Rebecca was betting his oversized ego had suffered the most damage. She still wasn't ready to excuse his deplorable behavior, but the frost inside her thawed a few degrees. She could only imagine how crushing it had been for a prideful man like Hank Abernathy to woo a woman who'd ultimately deemed him to be unworthy of her.

"Spoiled debutantes living in big houses don't deserve such sentiments." Hank Abernathy's voice wafted out from beneath his hat, making his listeners aware he'd only been pretending to sleep. He lounged deeper into the seat, crossing and uncrossing his legs. "Fear not. My heart remains unscathed."

The sarcasm rolling off of him made Rebecca's face turn red. Not every young woman living in a big house was overindulged and insensitive to the feelings of others. She and Hope were proof of that. At least, they strived to be kind. Indignation rolled through her, propelling her to lash back at him. "The unscathed part I can easily believe. You'd have to first possess a heart for it to be broken."

Stunned silence met her outburst.

Hope appeared to be having trouble breathing, but a snicker escaped Pete. "Truer words were never spoken." He used the toe of his boot to nudge his friend's boot, looking like he wanted to say more. However, he refrained.

A porter bustled their way with a tray of beverages balanced on an upraised arm. As he reached their seats, the train lurched, making him stumble. The tray tilted and slid sideways. For the space of a few heartbeats, it teetered over Hope's head.

Pete Bishop lunged in her direction and caught the tray before it finished tipping over.

"Oh, thank you, sir!" The server swiveled dazedly in

their direction to identify his savior. Finding himself face-to-face with a tall, dark-skinned cowboy, his eyebrows shot heavenward. "It was you?"

Pete inclined his head respectfully. "My pleasure, sir." He pressed the tray back into the man's hands and returned to his seat as if nothing unusual had occurred.

"You are everything that is kind, sir. We are in your debt." Rebecca smiled warmly across the narrow walkway at him, unable to continue holding his unfortunate relationship with Hank Abernathy against him.

"You were so quick on your feet." Hope's gaze sparkled with gratitude. "My borrowed gown thanks you. As do I."

Over the course of the next several hours, Rebecca learned that Hank Abernathy and Pete Bishop were weary of the wounds that the war had inflicted on the south. They were finished working with plantation owners who couldn't see beyond Hank's humble beginnings or the color of Pete's skin. They were venturing west with their horse breeding business, in the hopes of settling in a town that would be more accepting of their diverse partnership.

"What kind of horses do you breed?" Hope's wide, almond-hued eyes snapped with interest.

Rebecca had never before seen her so attentive during a discussion about livestock. Normally, she only showed that level of animation over topics like fabric colors and fashion. She was highly skilled with a needle and thread, having both designed and constructed the very dress Rebecca had insisted she borrow for their journey. If their stint in teaching didn't go as planned, she had the potential to become a professional seamstress.

"Missouri Fox Trotters mostly." Pete watched her closely for her reaction. When he received a blank look, he shook his head. "You've never heard of them, have you?"

"We were raised on a cotton farm," Rebecca interjected dryly. Hope had spent a good part of her childhood working in the fields. "The horses we're accustomed to are the kind that pull wagons and carriages."

"Ah." He nodded. "Thoroughbreds, I reckon."

"Yes." She saw no need to elaborate, since her family's wealth was a thing of the past. However, her father had owned a dozen or more horses at any given time. He was a connoisseur of horseflesh and had acquired the best on the market for her and her brothers to ride and for Ezekiel to hitch to their carriage.

"Missouri Fox Trotters are a special breed," Pete declared proudly. "They're known for their smooth, four-beat gait. If you ever have the pleasure of riding one, you won't want to go back to riding a horse with a two-beat gait. It's a much smoother, more comfortable ride."

"It sounds lovely." Hope smiled wistfully. While spending her childhood as a slave, she hadn't enjoyed the luxury of riding horses. As a result, she was vastly intimidated by the creatures. Thus far, Rebecca had been unable to coax her to ride. "Not that I have any experience in the matter."

His sooty brows drew together. "You mean you've never ridden a horse before?" His gaze dropped to her hands, and he abruptly cleared his throat. "I would be happy to give you a riding lesson sometime."

From the corner of her eye, Rebecca watched Hope curl her hands into the fabric of her gown and wished she'd thought to lend her a pair of gloves. During the emotion-charged hubbub of leaving her childhood home, she'd all but forgotten how sensitive Hope was about the scars her hands would forever bear from her slave days.

Rebecca waited until Pete Bishop looked away before

discreetly sliding her own gloves off and slipping them, balled-up, to Hope.

Hope sent her a grateful look and just as discreetly slid them over her hands.

OVER THE NEXT SEVERAL DAYS, PETE BISHOP PROVED TO be an entertaining travel companion, regaling Rebecca and Hope with one story after another about the horses he and Hank had acquired or bred, trained, and sold. They worked with farmers and ranchers all across the southeastern seaboard, but now they were branching westward.

Hank Abernathy spent a lot of time sleeping or pretending to sleep. When he was awake, he all but ignored Rebecca and Hope. No matter how hard his partner tried to draw him into their conversations, he chose to remain aloof and detached.

Rebecca tried to ignore him in return, but it was difficult. She kept replaying their initial conversation in her head and couldn't come up with a reasonable explanation for how she'd offended him. It was as if he found her very existence objectionable. She contented herself, instead, with counting the hours until they reached their destination.

Which they finally did.

The moment their train nosed into the Cedar Falls Train Depot she was able to breathe easier. She stared raptly through the window and came to one very quick conclusion. The train was arriving at the end of a line. It would have to depart the same way it had arrived.

The dismal thought popped into her mind that their

new venture might turn out to be just as much of a dead end. Questions flooded her, tightening her insides with apprehension.

What will happen to us when our temporary teaching positions end? Where will we go next? But first things first. They needed to figure out where they would reside during their stay in Cedar Falls. The mayor had mentioned something about sending a wagon to transport their belongings to an inn or a boarding house. She leaned closer to the window, anxiously searching the array of wagons and carriages on the other side of the train platform. She hoped he kept his word, since their journey to Texas had put a sizable dent in her savings. It wouldn't stretch much further before she and Hope received their first paychecks.

Hope reached for her hand as they stood to disembark. Both were travel rumpled and clutching reticules. She leaned closer to murmur, "We're in good hands with Mr. North. I can feel it in my bones."

Rebecca wished she shared her friend's optimism, but all she was feeling at the moment was the weight of uncertainty. "I pray you are right," she returned breathlessly. "We have nowhere else to go." Nor anyone else to turn to.

Feeling the itch of awareness between her shoulder blades, she darted a glance over her shoulder and discovered Hank Abernathy standing directly behind her. He was wearing an arrested expression that was very much at odds with the aloof manner he'd exhibited up to this point.

Their gazes clashed and held, sending an inexplicable thrill through her. For a split second, she wished they'd never disagreed over her comment about his Irish ancestry. Or whatever else he'd taken offense to. The source of his discontentedness remained a mystery to her.

He scanned her features, and his expression grew shut-tered again. The moment they'd been sharing was gone.

Rebecca raised her chin and returned her attention to Hope, sweeping up the aisle at her side. Together, they stepped through the doorway leading to the train platform.

"Oh, my!" Her breath caught in her throat at the tall, stalwart cedar trees dotting the sides of the road and the gently rolling landscape on either side of them. The luscious evergreens provided a stunning view. It was no wonder the founding settlers had named their town after them.

Quaint storefront buildings rose in front of them — tidy, well-maintained, and bustling with activity. The building to Rebecca's right housed a sawmill. Her nose detected the scent of freshly cut wood and the dusty overtones of sawdust. Behind her, she could hear the metal clang of a blacksmith at work. The cacophony of muted sounds blended in a backdrop that was peaceful, comforting, and inviting. She filled her lungs with fresh air, willing her insides to unknot.

Someone bumped into her from behind, jarring her from her thoughts and nearly sending her to her knees. If Hope hadn't been holding so tightly to her hand, Rebecca would've gone sprawling.

She cast a startled look around them and caught sight of a man in overalls sprinting down the steps of the platform. "He's certainly in a hurry!" Regardless, it was rude of him to plow so carelessly into her. Her shoulder was still smarting from the impact. She instinctively reached for the strap of her reticule.

It was missing! The blood left her face at the realization that the remainder of her small savings was also missing. Her gaze returned frantically to the running man as he made a sharp right at the base of the platform and headed down the street. Though it was difficult to make out the details with any clarity, he appeared to be clutching something in front of him.

"What's troubling you, dearest?" Hope's hand tightened on hers.

Before Rebecca could form an answer, Pete Bishop's kind voice washed over them. "Please assure us you ladies didn't intend to leave without a proper farewell."

She whirled blindly in his direction.

"What's wrong?" He sounded aghast.

"My reticule." She pointed shakily at the fleeing man. "I believe that man stole it. The one wearing overalls."

Pete Bishop and Hank Abernathy exchanged a swift, hard look. Then they tossed their travel bags at her and Hope's feet.

"Keep an eye on these," Hank commanded harshly. Without waiting for so much as a nod of acquiescence from her, he sprinted after the man in overalls. Pete was right beside him.

The man they were pursuing didn't get far. Rebecca winced as Hank and Pete caught up to him. Hank tackled him first, sending the shabby creature tumbling to the ground. Fists flew, and a few shouted words were exchanged. Then the man in overalls rolled to his feet and took off running again. This time, Hank and Pete didn't pursue him. They jogged back to the train platform where Rebecca and Hope were waiting.

"Here." Hank held out Rebecca's reticule.

She reached for it, fighting tears as she hugged it close. "Thank you! We're in your debt."

"Indeed you are," he agreed coolly. "We'll be sure to collect when the time is right."

Pete snorted out a laugh, rolling his shoulders a few times. "What Hank is trying to say is, the fellow who robbed you won't be bothering you anymore."

It wasn't at all what Hank had said, but Rebecca let it go. She was too shaken to be drawn into another bickering match with his cranky business partner.

"Who was that man?" Hope glanced worriedly in the direction he'd limped off to, but he was no longer in sight.

"A no-good scallawag," Pete growled. "From the way he was dressed, I'd peg him for a farm hand. Poor and hungry, no doubt, but that's no reason to assault a lady."

We're poor, too. Rebecca found the entire situation sad, unfortunate, and unsettling. "It all happened so quickly." She struggled to collect herself. She wasn't sure what would've become of them if Hank and Pete hadn't recovered her precious savings. She and Hope might've found themselves sleeping on the street tonight!

Hank raised an eyebrow at her wrinkled mourning gown. "He probably figured a woman dressed like you would have coins to spare."

She blinked to hold back angry tears, knowing nothing could be further from the truth. Nothing! He deserved to have his ears boxed for constantly assuming the worst about her. No matter what she looked like to him, she wasn't a pampered rich woman begrudging a hungry thief his next meal. On the contrary, the money he'd stolen from her might very well be the only thing keeping her and Hope from starving in the coming days!

"Well, then." Pete tipped his hat gallantly at them. "I reckon this is goodbye. For now, at least." He winked at Hope. "There's still the matter of your riding lesson to discuss once we get settled in at the ranch."

The ranch. His words had a lovely ring to them. Envy

welled in Rebecca, threatening to consume her. It was ironic that a grumpy former indentured servant and the pleasant former slave at his side would soon be enjoying the comforts of home.

While Hope and I scrounge for the cheapest place we can find to sleep for the night. Surely a town this small would have accommodations in their price range. They would be looking for something dirt cheap.

Hope sent Pete a sunny smile, observing him from beneath half-lowered lashes. "I like the sound of that, sir." She had yet to call him or Hank by their first names.

"Pete," he corrected. "I insist. It's only fitting after such a long and arduous journey together that we part as friends."

"An excellent idea, Pete." Hope impulsively held out a hand. "I welcome the notion of starting off with a friend or two in town." She cast an uncertain look in Hank's direction, clearly seeking his affirmation.

He either didn't notice or pretended not to. He was too busy gawking at Rebecca again. His piercing blue gaze engaged in a silent duel with hers. After a moment of strained silence amongst the four of them, he gave her a rigid nod and bent to retrieve his travel bag at her feet.

"Miss Copeland! Miss Thompson!" A silver-haired man wearing a navy suit hurried up the stairs to join them on the platform. "You made it!" He sounded so cheerful and welcoming that it came as no surprise when he introduced himself as Mayor Reggie North.

Hank paused for a moment to observe their encounter, making no effort to hide his smirk. No doubt he considered the mayor's exuberant welcome as yet more proof of Rebecca's uppityness. Not that she cared what he thought.

Oh, who am I trying to fool? She gritted her teeth at the

unfortunate realization that she did indeed care. It made no sense. He'd certainly given her no reason to care, but she did.

Her inability to turn off the wistful feeling rankled. Deeply.

Chapter 3: Not Adding Up
Hank

Hank watched the lovely Rebecca Copeland and her exotically dark travel companion as they were ushered by the mayor into an awaiting carriage. A white-haired woman was seated inside, dressed every inch as fashionably as they were. *That figures!* He turned away in disgust from the expensive-looking rig with its gold-painted M over the door. Though Rebecca had nearly fooled him with her white-faced fear and teary response to the robbery incident, his earlier suspicions about her slammed back into place.

She was a wealthy southern belle — his least favorite segment of the population, a woman who'd foolishly risked life and limb to travel west without a proper escort. It was ill-advised of her on every level. Her stolen reticule was proof of that. What sort of father had allowed her to go gallivanting off like that? Or brothers? Or cousins? Hank gnashed his teeth. It wasn't likely he would ever meet the rest of her family, which was a good thing since he wanted to throttle every last one of them.

Furthermore, he wasn't the least bit bamboozled by her

attempt to pass off Hope Thompson as a gently bred woman. He'd gotten an eyeful of her scarred and callused hands before she'd had the wherewithal to hide them beneath a pair of gloves. He was guessing she was a former slave, which in no way explained the depth of affection between the two women. Had Hope once belonged to Rebecca? Before the war, perhaps?

The possibility that Rebecca had once been a slave owner turned his stomach. It would mean she and her family had lorded over people like him and Pete. Just like another southern belle he was trying his hardest to forget — a heartless beauty who'd been quick to flirt with him when they were alone and equally quick to snub him in the presence of her friends. She'd made him feel like the dirt beneath her fancy dancing shoes.

Yet here he was — attracted to yet another beautiful, educated, wealthy woman. From the first moment he'd made eye contact with Rebecca Copeland, he'd felt the magnetic pull between them. To make matters worse, the feeling was stronger than anything he'd ever experienced, which he could only hope wouldn't become a problem for them. It was way too bad she and Hope would be living in the same town as him and Pete. With any luck, the circles they moved in would make them easier to avoid.

Pete nudged him with his shoulder as the carriage rolled away, taking Rebecca and Hope out of their lives, possibly for good. "Are you alright? You look like you sank your teeth into a rotten apple."

"That's one way of putting it." Hank grimaced as they strode with their travel bags toward the car carrying their livestock. The porters were just now starting to unload the animals. It hadn't been easy or cheap to bring their favorite mounts, but he and Pete owned a few horses they'd been unable to part with. It would be another couple of weeks before their next shipment of Missouri Fox Trotters arrived. By then, they would be settled in at their ranch and ready to get back to work.

A loud nickering sound alerted him to the fact that his stallion, a reddish-brown beast named Red Sabbath, finally had his hooves back on the ground. In a fun quirk of nature, Red Sabbath's glossy mane was the shade of freshly tossed straw.

"Hello, old friend." Hank held out his arms to the creature as the porter led him his way.

Red Sabbath nearly pulled the reins from the porter's hands in his haste to reach Hank.

"I'll take it from here." Hank accepted the reins from the porter, who was all too happy to receive his tip and be on his way.

"I just finished watering 'em and feeding 'em," he called over his shoulder before disappearing inside the train car once again.

He led Pete's horse, Titan, out next. The black stallion stood nearly as tall as Red Sabbath. Catching sight of Pete, he trumpeted out a greeting and reared back on his hind legs, scissoring his front hooves in the air.

The porter dropped the reins and leaped back a few steps to get out of the way. Another pair of porters hurried forward with whips in hand.

"Stop!" Hank and Pete shouted in unison, making the men skid to a halt.

"He's just anxious to stretch his legs." Hank stepped closer with Red Sabbath's reins in hand, knowing his horse's presence would go a long way toward calming the other stallion. "They've been cooped up for too long is all."

The porters backed away, looking rattled by the incident. One of them ominously cracked his whip in warning at the horse, earning him one of Hank's darkest glares. Fortunately, his and Pete's stallions were too well trained to react to such nonsense. They had their owners back, and they had each other. They knew they were safe.

As Hank and Pete led their horses a few paces away, Pete waggled his eyebrows at Hank. "You still look like you took a bite of something rotten."

Hank huffed out a breath, wishing his partner would let it go. However, he'd clearly been enamored with the two beautiful women sitting across from them during the train ride. Hank angled his head in the direction they had departed. "Mark my words. Rebecca and Hope aren't what they appeared to be."

"You mean lovely?" Pete gave him a wide smile that revealed his gleaming white teeth. "They became even lovelier as we became better acquainted." Whether he meant to or not, he puffed out his chest a little as he reflected on the progress he'd made getting to know them better.

"They're hiding something," Hank growled. "I'm not swallowing their story about their so-called divine calling to teach." He spat on the ground, trying to rid his mouth of the bad taste left there by Rebecca's snide remarks. "Not with the cut of the gowns they were wearing. My gut says something else is afoot. Nothing good, that's for sure."

His friend's expression grew troubled. "Although I agree everything about them didn't add up, I'm not convinced there's anything ominous in play. Both of them were pleasant. Genuinely pleasant. The kind of pleasant that a person can't fake."

"If by pleasant, you mean full of sass," Hank muttered, not ready to cease his grumbling. Something about Rebecca Copeland had gotten under his skin and stayed there. So much that he wasn't going to get a moment's peace of mind until they changed the subject. Maybe not even then.

"Only one of them was full of sass," Pete retorted cheerfully. "You may have finally met your match."

Since Hank was ready to talk about something else — literally anything else — he didn't bother pointing out that his obvious admiration for Hope was clearly blinding his assessment of Rebecca. In stark contrast to her travel companion, Hope was a shy, diminutive princess. There was strength in her, though. He'd sensed it right beneath the surface. No one could've survived what she and her people had endured without it.

Sadly, none of what she'd endured changed the fact that folks like Rebecca Copeland would continue to look down their noses at folks like Hank Abernathy. He could probably buy and sell her family's plantation a dozen times over, but beautiful, well-connected women never seemed to care how hard a man worked to make something of themselves. The moment they caught wind of Hank's humble beginnings, it was always the same story. He was relegated to the dredges of humanity they considered beneath their notice.

He'd found out the hard way. The first woman he'd fallen for had mailed him a mountain of sweetly penned letters throughout the war. She'd made countless promises to wait for his return. She'd lied, of course. By the time he'd straggled home from battle, she was already married to the son of her father's closest friend. She hadn't even bothered to inform Hank. He'd discovered the truth after attempting to surprise her with an engagement ring.

He reached up to trace the scar her father had left on his face with his leather whip. Technically, the man hadn't wielded it himself. He'd paid a group of thugs to do his dirty work for him. Years later, their warnings continued to ring in his ears.

"You ain't good enough for her and never will be."

He'd vowed on the spot to never again court a wealthy woman. His scar was a reminder of that vow every time he looked in a mirror.

He and Pete kept their horses calm while the rail yard attendants completed the arduous task of unloading the rest of their earthly goods. It had taken multiple train cars to contain it all — a costly transport, but it was one they could easily afford. They'd brought their work wagon plus their nicer carriage. They'd also brought a slew of ranching gear — saddles, cinches, lead ropes, and grooming tools. It was everything they needed for the care and upkeep of the horses that would soon fill their new stables.

They'd sold off their other livestock before leaving Atlanta, so they would need to replace their cattle, chickens, and goats as soon as possible. In addition to their stallions, they'd retained possession of their brood mares and a pair of foals. There was no need to start from scratch after working so hard to acquire the highest quality horses in the country.

The owner of the ranch they were purchasing arrived before their belongings were fully unloaded. Stanley West-field was a bald man with a shaggy white mustache. From the leathery lines crisscrossing his face, he could've been seventy or a hundred and seventy. It was impossible to pinpoint the ages of most of the sun-dried ranchers they encountered.

Mr. Westfield waved away the offer of assistance from his driver in lieu of climbing down from his carriage alone. Once his feet were on the ground, he took a few stumbling steps and had to pause to regain his equilibrium. A second man climbed down after him. He wore a charcoal pinstriped suit and carried a pretentious walking stick.

Hank only half listened to the introductions. As it turned out, Mr. Walking Stick was the town banker, Percy Randolf. He announced in a much louder voice than necessary that he would be accompanying them on their initial tour of the ranch, after which they would finalize the purchase.

Hank and Pete got to work loading their wagon and carriage, hitching a team of horses to each of them. They tied the foals behind the rigs, which would require them to drive slowly. Since it wouldn't hurt to have an extra pair of hands while moving into their new place, Hank jogged to the livery a few doors down the street to hire the services of a groom for the day.

The fresh-faced lad took one look at their Missouri Fox Trotters and started beaming. He smoothed his hand down their noses and spoke to each of them before they departed.

Mr. Westfield's driver led their caravan toward his ranch, which Hank and Pete would soon rename to A & B Horse Ranch. Hank couldn't wait to have a sign commissioned that would double as an advertisement for their horse breeding business.

They passed through the downtown area of Cedar Falls, a crisscross of streets crammed with storefront buildings and pedestrians. Afterward, they set their course for the outskirts of town. Hank and Pete's new homestead was sprawled across a hundred and sixty acres of land.

The farmhouse drew into view, making his heart pound with excitement. The description in Mr. Westfield's letters hardly did the place justice. For one thing, the house was bigger than he'd been expecting — two-and-a-half stories with lots of windows and a wrap-around porch.

Mr. Westfield had his driver slow down and pull to one side so Hank could draw his wagon abreast of it on one side while Pete pulled their carriage abreast of it on the other side. The aging rancher pointed out the highlights of the property. "There's another farmhouse a few acres over, not quite as large as this one. We built it for our daughter and son-in-law, hoping to move them out this way, but we couldn't talk them into leaving San Francisco." He lifted his hat and scratched his head before settling it back in place. "That's where my wife and I are heading next. There's no point in fighting the inevitable." He let out a gusty whoosh of resignation. "Her heart is with our three grandchildren, and a fourth one on the way. She'll have me tarred and feathered if I drag my heels any longer."

Hank appreciated hearing the Westfields' reason for moving. It meant he and Pete wouldn't need to spend the rest of the afternoon searching exhaustively for items in poor repair to haggle a better price. The homestead rising in front of them showed every sign of having been loved and cared for.

They pulled their caravan in a semi-circle in front of the farmhouse and soon discovered that the interior of the home was as attractive and inviting as the exterior. The paint and wallpaper looked fresh, and the furniture was in good repair. The best part about it was that most of the pieces would stay with the house. The Westfield's were relocating to a smaller home, which had made them eager to negotiate many of their belongings into the selling price.

While the hired groom kept a watchful eye on the horses, Hank and Pete joined Mr. Westfield and Mr. Randolf for a tour of the property. It contained two barns, three ponds, and the second farmhouse Mr. Westfield had previously mentioned. It was only a story and a half, but it was equally well cared for and furnished.

After a quick tour, Hank and Pete stepped outside on the back porch.

"I could see myself staying here." Pete rocked back on the heels of his boots, slinging his thumbs through his belt loops.

"We could add on to it, I reckon." Hank hadn't seen any point in dickering over who slept where before they laid eyeballs on the property. "Fancy it up to match the other house."

"I think I like it just the way it is," his partner drawled. "It's nicer than the last place we shared, and I'd have it all to myself."

"Not for long, if Winifred Monroe has anything to say about it," Hank reminded dryly. He was surprised the spinster owner of the Cedar Falls Rail Yard hadn't been present to greet them upon their arrival in town. She'd been excessively vocal in her letters and telegrams to them before their trip, personally handling the details concerning the transport of their livestock and belongings. They had an appointment with her tomorrow to settle their final bill.

Her excessive vocalness had extended to an offer to find him and Pete wives. After they'd ignored that part of her letter, she'd written again to assure them she already had the perfect two ladies in mind.

He'd never before met a woman as outspoken as Ms. Monroe. Then again, he'd never before met a woman who owned a rail yard. As crazy as it sounded, a small part of him had been tempted to take her up on her offer to select wives for them. Installing a bride at A & B Ranch sooner rather than later would've been a sure-fire way of getting things done quickly — everything from home decorating to starting a family.

After meeting Rebecca Copeland, however, he no longer found much humor in the thought of the town busy-body picking out a wife for him like a pair of boots from a catalogue. No matter how hard he tried, he couldn't stop thinking about Rebecca's graceful hand movements, her gentle southern accent, or her solid black gown. For mourning, he presumed. Mourning for whom, though? During the long journey to Texas, neither she nor Hope had shed an ounce of light on whoever Rebecca had lost.

Which hadn't stopped him from wondering. And feeling sorry for her, despite his every effort not to have any feelings at all for her.

While cutting through the farmhouse to the front porch, he forced himself to look into the next mirror he encountered. Ducking his head to look at his reflection, he fingered the scar on the left side of his face.

Never forget.

He couldn't afford to. Forcing his thoughts about the stunning Rebecca Copeland from his mind, he turned to his business partner. "Are you ready to take the leap?" He spoke quietly, so as not to be overheard by the aging rancher or the watchful banker. The sale of the ranch wasn't a done deal until he and Pete placed their signatures on the final document, accepting the condition they'd found the place in.

Pete made a shooting motion with his thumb and fore-finger, pretended to cock it and making a popping sound when it exploded.

It was all the encouragement Hank needed. He caught Mr. Westfield's eye. "All we need to do is make sure the groom outside is alright being alone with the horses for an hour or two. Then we'll follow you to the bank to sign the rest of the paperwork."

As expected, the expressions of both gentlemen creased into lines of confusion. Mr. Walking Stick was the first to recover. "I, er, that is...we assumed the other feller with you was, er..."

"The hired help?" Hank clapped Pete companionably on the back. "Not at all. *The other feller* is my business partner. He also happens to be one of the best horse trainers in the country. I believe one of you mentioned earlier that the reputation of our Missouri Fox Trotters preceded us to Texas?" He raised a challenging eyebrow at them, daring them to deny it.

After an uncomfortable pause, Mr. Westfield nodded so vehemently that his Stetson nearly tumbled to the floor. He caught it and pushed it more firmly back on his head. "So long as you have the money, I don't reckon it matters who makes the purchase." His lips flattened into a thin line. "My wife might not be too thrilled about who's staying in the house intended for our daughter and her family, but..." He gave a rigid nod in Pete's direction. "As of this evening, we'll be staying at the Cedar Falls Inn. So long as we keep this business between us men," he waggled a finger between them, "she'll be none the wiser for it."

It was all Hank could do not to send a balled fist through the man's jaw. In the end, it was a warning head shake from Pete that prevented it. Under the guise of examining a built-in bookshelf more closely, he muttered in Hank's ear, "Let it go, brother. Just let it go."

Hank purposely walked with Pete several paces behind the other two men as they followed them outside and up the hard-packed dirt lane to the main farmhouse. "That kind of talk is everything we thought we were leaving behind in Atlanta," he snarled in a low voice.

"The Westfields aren't from Texas," Pete reminded mildly. "He said so himself. They moved here from the east coast in search of wide-open skies, and now they're giving it up to return to city life. All griping aside about what his wife might or might not think about two men she's never going to meet, their loss feels like our tremendous gain." He spread his hands to take in the gently rolling acreage on either side of them. "To God be the glory!"

Hank nodded grudgingly. Having been orphaned at an early age in Ireland and sold by an ailing uncle into indentured servitude at the age of thirteen, he'd never been much of a religious man himself. He'd not seen any evidence of God's grace in his uncle or most of the people he'd encountered afterward. Despite the lens of faith through which Pete chose to view everything, it was a dog-eat-dog world. Hank was convinced the only reason he and Pete had survived was by sticking together. They'd been doing it for more than a decade now.

Pete had somewhat restored Hank's faith in humanity by stealing away with Hank's unit and following him to war. The only reason he'd been allowed to remain by Hank's side was because he'd posed as his servant. By the time they'd returned to Atlanta, Pete had been emancipated. Even then, they'd been uninterested in parting ways, using Hank's savings from his soldier's pay to go into business together.

They'd started out working in a few rented stalls at a local livery. A few years later, they'd grown into a thriving business in an old warehouse that had doubled as their bunkhouse.

Now here we are.

They'd come a long way, and Hank was as thrilled about it as Pete was. He just wasn't convinced God had much to do with it. However, since giving God the glory for everything seemed to make Pete sleep better at night, Hank didn't intend to argue the point.

———

SIGNING THE PAPERWORK AT THE BANK DIDN'T TAKE near as long as Hank expected, which was a good thing. He didn't like leaving their horses alone with a stranger for too long, albeit one who'd come so highly recommended at the livery.

In less than an hour, he and Pete were holding the keys to their new homestead. Pete waited until they were clear of the busy downtown streets and riding toward the outskirts of town again before giving a crow of delight. Titan tossed his head and trumpeted back like he understood.

"It's just me, you loco horses," Pete scolded good-naturedly, and they settled back into a steady trot.

Hank grinned over his partner's burst of exuberance. He was experiencing the same sense of elation. The same giddy burst of pride. Not too many years ago, they'd been scrawny lads that no one expected would amount to much.

And look at us now!

They exchanged gleeful grins.

"We have a home, Hank!" There was a hitch of emotion in Pete's voice that Hank had never heard before. "A real one. And it's all ours."

"It's all ours," Hank echoed, liking the taste and feel of the words in his mouth. There'd be no more rented stalls for them. No more dusty warehouses. No more hot and drafty lofts in which to hang their hats and spread out their bedrolls for a few nights. No, sir. They would be sleeping on real mattresses in real beds from now on.

Though he didn't particularly want to, his thoughts returned to the elegant southern belle he'd journeyed to Cedar Falls with, along with her shy travel companion. Wherever Rebecca and Hope were staying tonight, there was no way it was any nicer than the homestead he and Pete had just purchased. It had taken far more than money to reach this milestone. It had cost them years of blood, sweat, and tears, which made it all the more satisfying.

Tomorrow, he and Pete would celebrate over lunch with the hoity-toity Ms. Winifred Monroe, who would undoubtedly renew her efforts to marry them off as quickly as possible. He still didn't know who she had in mind for their prospective brides, but he imagined they were about to find out.

Regardless of who the future Mrs. Hank Abernathy ended up being, one thing was certain. She would have a fine farmhouse to preside over with one of the finest views in the country. His bride would have no cause to avert her gaze or hang her head around women of Miss Copeland's ilk. No, indeed. He and Pete were moving up in the world, and there wasn't a blessed thing folks like her could do to stop them.

Chapter 4: Delightful Interference
Rebecca

Rebecca was exhausted in body and soul from the train ride and the robbery that had nearly separated her from the rest of her small savings. However, that didn't keep her from enjoying the surprisingly elegant cobblestone road their hostess's driver turned the carriage on. It was lined on both sides by towering green cedars that blocked the sun, providing immediate relief from the summer heat.

As it turned out, the mayor hadn't met them at the train station to transport them and their belongings to the nearest inn after all. There'd been a change of plans since the last letters they'd exchanged. An aging member of the school board was hosting them in her home instead. A tiny white-haired spinster bearing the name of Winifred Monroe. The same woman who'd promised to find wives for the tall, dark, and handsome Pete Bishop and his dreadfully cocky business partner. As badly as Rebecca didn't want to have anything to do with the self-proclaimed matchmaker, she'd been unable to turn down such a generous offer for accommodations.

Ms. Monroe waved a heavily be-ringed hand at the scene unfolding outside the windows of her carriage. "Our town was named after these trees." Both pride and affection rang in her voice. "When the land started getting built up, I made sure the mayor passed a resolution to plant a new cedar tree every time the loggers cut one down."

"It was very wise of you, ma'am." Rebecca caught Hope's eye and found her biting her lower lip to hold in a smile. She was obviously having no trouble imagining the opinionated Ms. Monroe telling the mayor what to do. Despite her outspoken manner, the elderly lady was impeccably garbed in a summer gown as white as her hair. The fabric was embroidered with delicate wildflowers. A pearl choker circled her neck, and matching pearl teardrops dangled from her ears.

"It was necessary," she stated in a succinct, no-nonsense voice. "Sometimes politicians get so caught up in lofty matters, they forget the common-sense initiatives."

Rebecca finally gave up the fight to remain serious and smiled at their benefactor. "I applaud your efforts. I truly do. I also want to thank you again for inviting us to spend our first night in town with you. It's so generous." It was more than generous. It was everything that was kind and considerate to save them the cost of a room at the inn.

Ms. Monroe's welcoming smile twisted into a frown. "Who said anything about one night?"

Rebecca gaped at her, trying to comprehend what she'd said to cause offense. "I suppose I just assumed, ma'am—"

Ms. Monroe broke into a delighted cackle. "But of course you did!" She cackled some more. "To be more clear, I wish for you and Miss Thompson to stay a spell with me."

A spell? Rebecca was more confused than ever. "We wouldn't want to impose on you, ma'am."

Ms. Monroe gave an unladylike snort. "When you see my home, you'll understand how foolish that sounds."

Oh, my! Rebecca stared wide eyed out the window until a sprawling ranch house came into view. It seemed that Ms. Monroe had been referring to the sheer enormity of the place. A wide veranda spanned the white adobe front of her home. It wrapped around the first story on both sides, looking like it disappeared straight into the forest of cedar trees on either side of it. The second story had as many windows as the first story, plus two balconies. A lengthy two-story addition on each side turned the structure into a giant U shape.

Hope's gasp of surprise drew a chuckle of delight from Ms. Monroe. "Welcome to Bent Horseshoe Ranch," she announced grandly. "As you can see, it will be no imposition at all to house two lovely ladies for as long as you wish."

Rebecca's lips parted in astonishment. "For as long as we wish, ma'am?"

"For as long as you wish, my dears." Ms. Monroe seemed to be enjoying their puzzlement. "Ever since my niece, Anna Kate, married and moved out, it's been way too quiet around here."

"Are you certain it won't be too much trouble?" Rebecca was half afraid she'd fallen asleep and was dreaming up the entire conversation. It felt way too good to be true. "I caught a glimpse of the Cedar Falls Inn on our way here—"

"Nonsense!" Ms. Monroe's tone was emphatic. "It's no trouble at all. Though my brother and his sons are currently out of town on business, they'll be delighted to make your acquaintance upon their return." She briefly shared how they'd moved west to occupy her old carriage house and take over the day-to-day operations of her rail yard. "Leaving me to do whatever I please," she finished with another one of her infectious cackles. "And right now, it pleases me to host Cedar Falls' lovely newest guests."

Rebecca was momentarily at a loss for words.

Hope's soft voice filled in the silence. "Saying thank you feels inadequate, ma'am, but I'll say it, anyway. With all of my heart, I thank you."

Ms. Monroe's smile grew wider. "Your youthful companionship will bring some much needed life into the quiet walls of my home. That's all the thanks I need. Believe me. You'll understand when you get older."

The fact that she was so generously opening her home to both of them, without prejudice, proved to be Rebecca's undoing. The last people who'd been this accepting of Hope was her dearly departed family. As the driver brought the horses to a standstill, tears streaked from the corners of her eyes and rolled down her cheeks.

"There, there." Ms. Monroe produced a lacy handkerchief and held it out to her.

"You're an answer to our prayers, Ms. Monroe," she choked. "You have no idea how much." She hadn't yet told Hope that her savings would've only kept them at the inn for a week at most. Afterward, they would've been on the street.

"I have a better idea than you think." The woman's cryptic response made Rebecca blink. "My brother used to run one of the biggest rail lines in Atlanta. We have friends and associates all over the city you grew up in."

"Used to, ma'am?" Rebecca quavered. Unless she was mistaken, it sounded like the woman was well versed on the Copeland family's tragedies.

The aging spinster gave a short nod. "The war put a big dent in our business endeavors in Georgia. Enough that my brother, Jack, finally agreed to pull up his southern roots and transplant his children in Texas." Her expression softened. "Though it was a big adjustment for them at first, I can no longer imagine life without them." Her voice dripped with unadulterated adoration. "I can't wait to introduce you to them. Jackson is my oldest nephew. A true war hero who lost part of a leg to the cause." Her sigh of regret filled the carriage. "Not that it's kept the ladies in town from making a to-do over him. I expect he'll be wed to one of them by Christmas." There was no mistaking the indulgent affection in her voice.

Her chattering made Rebecca's thoughts drift to the two brothers she'd left at the cemetery in Marietta. She was only dimly aware of the carriage door opening, and Ms. Monroe's driver lifting her down.

It was only after her own feet touched the ground that she realized Ms. Monroe was seated in a wheelchair.

Rebecca dabbed at the dampness on her cheeks, at a loss for words all over again. Ms. Monroe was certainly full of surprises.

"Leave your trunks and travel bags," she commanded like a woman who was accustomed to being obeyed. "My butler will handle such matters." She gestured at the stately looking older gentleman whose gloved hands were resting on the handles of her chair. He was the same man who'd driven them to her home. "All you need to concern yourselves with is resting from your travels and washing up for dinner." She went on to promise that a maid would meet them in their rooms to draw baths for them. Another maid would air out and press the gowns in their travel bags.

"That sounds heavenly, ma'am." Hope sounded a trifle shaken, every ounce as overwhelmed as Rebecca was by the generosity of their hostess.

It felt like they were walking in a dream up the porch

steps and across the threshold of her impressive home. They followed Ms. Monroe and her driver down a massive center hallway, so spacious that it felt like it belonged in a castle. The guest suite she and Hope were deposited in was as big as the staff cottages dotting the plantation she'd grown up in.

Ms. Monroe spun her chair around, announcing they would be sharing the bedroom and its adjoining sitting area and powder room. "Though it was only a guess, I figured the two of you would be more comfortable staying together."

"Oh, for sure, ma'am," Rebecca agreed. "Hope is like a sister to me." Her instincts were telling her that Ms. Monroe already knew that to be the case. The more she heard Ms. Monroe talk, the more she was convinced that the woman's contacts in Atlanta had shared a good many details with her about the Copelands.

"We'll leave you to get settled in." A flick of Ms. Monroe's wrist caused her driver to roll her out of the room. He closed the door behind them, leaving them gaping in amazement at each other. He knocked on the door a few minutes later with a trio of servants in tow to deliver their travel bags and trunks to the room.

After he departed a second time, she and Hope traded a wide-eyed look and stepped into each other's arms.

"We're going to be alright," Hope declared damply. "The Lord already has the details worked out, just like I said He would."

"Your faith was greater than mine." Rebecca hugged her tightly. "I wanted to believe you, but it was...difficult." She'd never had to trust the Lord like this before. It was a new experience and a terrifying one, at that.

They ultimately skipped Ms. Monroe's suggestion to

rest. After being cooped up inside a train for days, it was a real treat to be able to stretch their legs again. They took turns bathing and helping each other button the backs of their gowns and style their hair. Then they followed their noses to the kitchen to offer their assistance with the food preparation.

Ms. Monroe's cook had a feast in the works. There was a ham in the oven, a covered pot of potatoes simmering on one side of the stove, and a pan of corn-on-the-cob boiling in saltwater on the other side. A loaf of bread was cooling on a nearby rack with a platter of preserves resting beside it.

Rebecca's mouth watered at the sight of the preserves. She mentally ticked off the flavors in her head — raspberry, peach, boysenberry, rhubarb, and pear. There was no doubt about it. Ms. Monroe lived like a queen.

Her dumpling of a cook shooed them away like flies. "If you insist on being underfoot, you may set the table." The most noteworthy thing about her scolding demeanor was that she didn't treat Hope any differently than Rebecca.

The second most noteworthy thing about the encounter was that the cook was in the midst of setting more food on the dining room table than three women could possibly eat by themselves. Rebecca hadn't seen so much food in one place since her parents had been alive. She and Hope had economized to painful levels afterward to make ends meet, sometimes sharing watered-down soup with nothing solid in it whatsoever.

"You really shouldn't have gone to so much trouble on our behalf," Rebecca murmured the moment Rupert rolled Ms. Monroe into the dining room. She was uncomfortably aware she couldn't repay the woman with a reciprocal dinner invitation, since she no longer had a home of her own. Maybe she would embroider a new handkerchief for her or extend some other small gesture.

"Pshaw!" Ms. Monroe waved away her comment. "Like you southern ladies, I've always enjoyed entertaining." She arched her white eyebrows knowingly at them.

Not any longer. It had been so long since the last time Rebecca had entertained visitors that she couldn't remember who she'd had over or what she'd served them. But Ms. Monroe didn't need to know that, so Rebecca swallowed her discomfort about the topic and forced a smile to her lips.

Ms. Monroe kept up a steady stream of chatter while they took their seats and settled their skirts around their chairs. Then she folded her hands in front of her. "Let us say grace." She bowed her head. "Dear heavenly Father..."

Rebecca's mind wandered tiredly during her long-winded prayer, wondering what had become of Hank Abernathy and his strappingly tall business partner. Were they staying at the inn this evening? Enjoying a sumptuous meal like she and Hope were about to? She wished she knew what part of town they planned to set up their horse training business in, but neither of them had volunteered the information. More than anything, Rebecca wondered when they would cross paths again.

Ms. Monroe ended her prayer before Rebecca was finished visualizing what her next encounter with the difficult Hank Abernathy would look like. Swallowing a sigh, she passed platters of food around the table, filling her plate with ham and vegetables. The meat was marinated and cooked to perfection with bits of pineapple dotting each slice.

"This is so good, ma'am." She briefly closed her eyes to savor it more fully.

"Everything is delicious," Hope chimed in happily. "Your cook really outdid herself, ma'am."

"I'll be sure to let her know." Ms. Monroe leaned forward in her chair. "Tell me about your plans, my dears. Your hopes. Your dreams. Don't leave anything out."

Silence settled over the table as Rebecca and Hope exchanged a wary glance.

"Everything?" Rebecca repeated cautiously. "You already know about our temporary teaching positions, of course."

"Of course." Ms. Monroe waved her slender hands dismissively. "Not to brag, but I single-handedly arranged all of that myself."

Rebecca was puzzled by her claim. "Naturally, we assumed it was the mayor's doing." He was the only person she'd corresponded with prior to boarding the train.

Ms. Monroe cackled loudly. "I dictated nearly every word of the letters he wrote to you."

"Then you are the perfect person to answer the rest of our questions, ma'am." Rebecca pounced eagerly on the opening the elderly woman had given them. "We'd love to know where the schoolhouse is, what sort of curriculum the teacher has been using, and anything else you deem pertinent to our jobs."

"About the schoolhouse..." Ms. Monroe's smile faded. "I'm sorry to report it caught on fire a few weeks ago. The wall nearest the wood stove was burnt to a skeleton. However, there's a pond around the bend, so the townsfolk were able to save the rest of the building and most of its contents. That said, it'll be under repairs for a while."

Rebecca's fork remained suspended in mid-air with a bite of ham on it. She couldn't bear the thought of having her and Hope's teaching contracts canceled before they could even begin work.

Ms. Monroe's mouth twisted into papery lines at the edges. "I can only imagine what you're thinking right now, but the mayor and I have come up with the perfect solution to the dilemma."

Hope reached beneath the table to clasp Rebecca's hand. "We're all ears, ma'am."

Ms. Monroe's smile returned in full force. "I'm offering the use of my drawing room for your temporary classroom, which is all the more reason for you to remain as my guests. Indefinitely."

Though Rebecca didn't object to working and living in such a lovely place, it seemed odd that no one had bothered writing to her and Hope about the change in venue. Since the fire had purportedly occurred weeks ago, there'd been more than enough time to send a telegram. Instead, the mayor and Ms. Monroe had waited until she and Hope had traveled over a thousand miles to share the news. Were they afraid she and Hope would change their minds?

As if that was even an option!

Ms. Monroe couldn't have looked or sounded more excited about the prospect of turning her home into a center of academic excellence. "The students are beside themselves with excitement at the notion of studying here." She warmed to the topic. "The rooms of my home are full of collectibles, photographs, centuries-old paintings, and more antiques than you can shake a stick at. In the spirit of learning, feel free to make use of it all."

"Please pardon the bluntness of my question, ma'am, but what's in it for you?" Rebecca wondered if the woman had calculated on the increased noise level that would surely come with the students, along with the very real possibility that something could get damaged.

"Nothing." Ms. Monroe beamed happily at them. "Absolutely nothing beyond the joy of contributing to my community. The Lord has been so good to me and my family. It's our turn to give back."

Rebecca studied her with new respect, sensing that Ms. Monroe was glossing over the fair share of trials she'd surely endured. The wheelchair she was sitting in was evidence of that.

You're trying to teach me something, Lord, aren't you? Maybe He hadn't abandoned her after all. She experienced a stab of guilt over the number of times she'd accused Him of that lately. Not in words, precisely, but in the unspoken resentment and bitterness she'd been harboring in her heart over the tremendous losses she'd suffered.

Despite her attitude, the Lord had seen fit to bring her and Hope into the luxurious home of an eccentric old lady. A woman who was generous to a fault. A woman who seemed determined to give them the time and space they needed to heal.

THE NEXT MORNING, THE CROW OF A ROOSTER JOSTLED Rebecca awake. "What a wonderful sound!" She stretched her arms over her head, yawning. She was thankful it was Saturday, giving her and Hope two full days to rest and settle into Cedar Falls before launching into their first day of teaching.

Hope made a mumbling sound and pulled her pillow over her face to muffle the sound.

"Such a slugabed!" Rebecca reached over to give her pillow a playful tug.

Hope held the pillow tighter over her head. "When I was a little girl," her voice came out muffled from beneath its downy thickness, "I dreamed of growing up to become a princess. And every last morning, the rooster crowed and chased away my dreams."

"After which you daydreamed about making him into stew, eh?" Many times, Rebecca had attempted to picture herself in Hope's shoes, but she'd been unable to do so.

Hope pushed the pillow aside and sat up. "Fortunately for him, his neck wasn't mine to wring."

Rebecca sat up beside her. "I'm sorry for all you and your family suffered."

Hope's eyes widened. "Look who's talking!"

"You know what I mean," Rebecca insisted with a wry shake of her head.

"Thanks to the Copelands, I haven't tasted hardship for many years." Hope's voice was firm. "You've always treated me like family, and I can't thank you enough for doing so."

Rebecca sniffed. "No hardship, says the friend who followed me straight out of the frying pan into the fire."

Hope leaned closer to bump shoulders with her. "Look around us, dearest. Even you would be hard put to call this a hardship."

Rebecca chuckled instead of answering. It was true. The suite of rooms they were staying in were every bit as nice as the ones in the mansion she'd left behind. The four-poster bed was piled with soft white linens, and gossamer white curtains framed a trio of picture windows. Their lacy hem draped all the way to the floor. A thick area rug covered the hardwood flooring, and every other comfort imaginable graced the rest of the rooms — a pair of ornately carved wardrobes, a writing desk, a blue-and-white striped chaise lounge, a brightly painted washbasin, and a bookshelf crammed with classical volumes.

Like Ms. Monroe herself, the rest of her home was a statement in refinement. The wood and tiled floors gleamed with cleanliness, and Rebecca didn't spot a single cobweb hanging from the chandeliers. There were jewel-toned rugs throughout the house, Queen Anne chairs, vases of flowers, paintings, collectible figurines, and so many shelves of beautifully bound books that she lost count of their numbers. The front parlor held a pianoforte just like the one she'd left behind. She could easily imagine gathering the school children around it for a singing fest.

It felt strangely like she'd been tossed right back into the paradise she'd been torn from — back when her life had been full of people and festivities, dinner parties and dances, picnics and musicales. Nostalgia pumped through her, making her fingers itch to coax a bit of music from the keys of the pianoforte.

Once upon a time, she'd been a skilled pianist, but it had been months since the last time she'd sat down to play. Too many months to count. The tragedies she'd suffered between then and now had silenced the very song in her heart.

Until now.

Rebecca gave the skirt of her black gown an irritated twitch. For the first time in months, the absence of color in her wardrobe troubled her.

"You and Hope may start teaching as soon as you like." Ms. Monroe's voice shattered her melancholy, bringing Rebecca back to the present — to the parlor they were gathered in.

This morning, their hostess had on a pair of reading

spectacles. A closed Bible was resting in her lap. "The children in town are clamoring to meet their new teachers. You know how children are. Always game for a new adventure." She smiled warmly at them over the top of her spectacles.

"I just assumed we'd get started on Monday." Rebecca paced the room, eyeing the titles of the volumes on the bookshelves. Ms. Monroe owned all the classics: Shakespeare, Dante, Homer, Keats, and Tennyson.

"If you feel rested enough by then." Ms. Monroe nodded in approval. "The children would be overjoyed to make your acquaintance so soon."

Hope spoke up from the velvet sofa, where she was seated with her hands folded. "How long have they been out of school, ma'am?"

"They haven't missed a lick of learning." The elderly woman fluttered a hand in the direction of downtown Cedar Falls. "There's a finishing school on the other side of town. It's run by Rachel and Boone Cassidy. They were quick to take the students in during the interim."

"A finishing school!" Rebecca hadn't expected to encounter anything of the sort in a town this small.

"You heard correctly." Ms. Monroe looked like she was enjoying being the bearer of such a juicy tidbit of news. "She's a hometown girl who got uprooted by a family member in Boston after her parents passed away. By the time she moved back to Cedar Falls, she was in possession of an inheritance that allowed her to snap up an old mansion and transform it into the Cedar Falls Finishing School for Young Ladies." She gave one of her happy cackles. "I can tell by your expressions what you're thinking, but she and her husband have made a real success of it. Word spread to the surrounding towns, and families from all over started sending their girls to the boarding school."

"I'm utterly fascinated!" It dawned on Rebecca that she'd sorely miscalculated the merits of moving to such a small town. Everywhere she turned, there was more than she'd been expecting — more businesses, more opportunities, and more good old-fashioned kindness. Cedar Falls was like a well-kept secret. With each passing minute, she wished they'd moved here sooner.

A knock sounded on the front door. Rebecca spun in surprise toward the sound. "I didn't know you were expecting company, ma'am." They'd finished their breakfast a mere half hour earlier. It was too soon for lunch guests.

"It's a small town where everybody knows everybody." Ms. Monroe returned airily as Rupert materialized to roll her wheelchair into the entry foyer. He appeared so quickly after the knocking started, and his presence was accompanied by no exchange of conversation with his mistress, leading Rebecca to believe that the two of them had, in fact, been expecting company.

Rupert was an imposing figure in a dark suit, with a ramrod spine and thinning gray hair. He swiftly wheeled Ms. Monroe to the front door and opened it. A murmur of male voices erupted on the other side.

While Ms. Monroe greeted her visitors, Rebecca finally gave in to the temptation to glide across the room to the pianoforte. She tentatively ran her fingers over the keys, drinking in the sound like a person dying of thirst.

"Do play something," Hope begged, rising to her feet and moving across the room to join her at the pianoforte. "It's been so long since I heard you play. Too long!"

With a sigh of capitulation, Rebecca perched on the round piano stool and hummed the lines of the first song that came to her mind. Then she plinked out the notes, filling the room with the age-old melody.

It was her mother's favorite church hymn, God Be With You. Her mother had sung it often while she was helping Hope's family escape north on the Underground Railroad.

After playing through the entry, Rebecca lifted her voice to sing out the lovely words of hope and promise.

> God be with you 'til we meet again.
>> God be with you 'til we meet again.
>> By His counsel's guide, uphold you,
>> With his sheep securely fold you;
>> God be with you 'til we meet again.

Hope's hands came down on her shoulders to rest warmly there while they sang the chorus together. Rebecca had no doubt Hope was seeing the beautiful faces of their loved ones again. Rebecca's father, Lincoln Copeland, and Hope's father, Jeremiah Thompson, men who'd defied their times to become friends.

As Rebecca sang, it felt like a moving tribute to their families. Her thoughts drifted to their mothers — Clara Copeland with her fancy dresses and bird-like laugh. No one in their social circle had suspected she had a serious enough bone in her body to be working so tirelessly behind the scenes to keep the Underground Railroad alive and running in their city. Likewise, no one who'd ever met Hope's mother would forget Hattie Thompson's sunny smiles and equally sunny temperament. She was always creating some new masterpiece or another with her needle and thread. Hope had inherited her gift for sewing beauty into the world.

> 'Til we meet, 'til we meet,
>> 'Til we meet at Jesus' feet;

'Til we meet, 'til we meet,
God be with you 'til we meet again.

A hushed silence filled the room when the last notes of the song faded. Though Rebecca raised her hands from the keys, her eyes remained closed while her heart paid homage to everyone she and Hope had lost or been forced to say goodbye to. Her cheeks were damp with tears, but she didn't bother brushing them away just yet. She wasn't ashamed of them. Her grief had become part of who she was.

The silence was broken at last by the slow, steady clapping of hands from the other side of the room.

Rebecca hastily scrubbed her cheeks dry and swiveled around on the stool to see who it was.

Her heart skipped a beat.

Hank Abernathy stood in the wide doorway leading from the entry foyer to the parlor. His upper lip was curled in his usual mocking half smile. "If we continue to cross paths like this, it's going to be difficult to believe it's nothing more than happenstance."

At first, all Rebecca could do was gape at him. If he was suggesting what she thought he was suggesting, he possessed no manners whatsoever. A hopeless cause. "You think *I* planned this visit?" She didn't bother hiding her anger or her sarcasm. His ego apparently knew no bounds.

To top it off, the crass cowpoke appeared to have no inkling he'd interrupted a private, heartfelt moment.

Pete edged around him to step farther into the room, studying Rebecca and Hope with concern. "Is everything alright? You ladies look sad."

Hope's fingers dug into Rebecca's shoulders. "No, er... we were simply, ah..."

63

Rebecca jumped back into the conversation to rescue her. "We were enjoying an impromptu musicale. That is all."

Pete nodded, still looking concerned. "What little I heard of it was marvelous." The frown on his forehead eased and was replaced by a look of admiration. "You sing beautifully. Both of you."

"Indeed, they do!" Rupert rolled Ms. Winifred Monroe's wheelchair back into the room. A harried expression was riding her classical features. "Pardon my lengthy absence from the room, but the milkman just arrived, and he's full of questions about the daily deliveries I requested for the school children."

"What a wonderful idea!" Her announcement made Rebecca realize she hadn't given much thought yet to the logistics of running a schoolroom. At the moment, her thoughts were in a frazzle due to Hank Abernathy's sudden appearance. She hadn't expected to see him again so soon, much less in this very room.

Ms. Monroe peered over her spectacles at Rebecca like she had earlier. "If you're sure you're ready to start on Monday, I'll let the milkman know to schedule his first bigger delivery then."

Yes, Rebecca was sure, but weren't there a few other steps they would need to take first? "Won't the school board want to meet us first, ma'am?" The same school board Ms. Monroe sat on? School teachers were normally quizzed about their moral fortitude before being released into the classroom. Or so Rebecca had been told. This was her first teaching position, so she didn't have any experience to go on.

Their hostess's lips twitched with humor. "Did Reggie honestly write that to you? I assured him it wasn't necessary after…" Her words dwindled, leaving Rebecca longing to hear the rest of her sentence.

After you did your own checking up on us, eh?

"But that's neither here nor there," Ms. Monroe added quickly. "All that matters is I have two of the loveliest ladies I've ever met in the same room as two of the handsomest gentlemen I've ever met." She made the introductions, not realizing how unnecessary it was, then gestured for Rupert to wheel her chair closer to the door. "Please continue getting to know each other, while I finish setting up our new delivery schedule with the milkman."

Mercy! The truth of what Ms. Monroe was really up to hit Rebecca like an avalanche. She felt the warmth of a blush creep up her neck as she twisted around on the piano stool to catch Hope's eye. The words of Mayor North's first letter came tumbling back to her.

Please don't be alarmed by what I'm going to write to you next, but it's only fair to warn you. One of our oldest board members takes particular delight in playing matchmaker, and it has been brought to her attention that the two of you are not yet betrothed.

Then there was Hank Abernathy's alarming statement about Winifred Monroe before they'd made the dear old lady's acquaintance — something about her picking out a pair of brides for him and Pete.

The way Hank's blue gaze was glittering with unholy glee told Rebecca that she'd correctly deduced what was happening. Ms. Monroe was attempting to play match-maker amongst the four of them.

In her agitation, she leaped up from the stool. "Please be

assured, Mr. Abernathy, that whatever you're thinking right now is most assuredly *not* going to happen."

Hope gave a soft whimper of warning, but the amusement in Hank's gaze merely deepened. "With all due respect, Miss Copeland, you have no idea what I'm thinking."

"Then let me make one thing clear," she snapped, feeling dangerously close to tears again. "The good Lord has called me to teach school, not fritter my time away on other...frivolous pursuits." It wasn't quite the turn of phrase she was looking for, but it was all she could come up with on the spot.

He nodded sagely. "By frivolous pursuits, I assume you're referring to..." He let the words hang in the air between them.

Her flush deepened. He was very aware she was referring to marriage — marrying *him*, to be more precise.

"Frivolous pursuits," he repeated, clearly enjoying her discomfort. "Such as braiding the tail of a horse or making a paper umbrella? Or..." He leaned around Hope to rasp, "to go skinny dipping?"

"Sir!" The word tore out of her in an agonized squeak.

He threw his hands into the air, feigning exasperation. "And we're back to formal titles. Make up your mind, Miss Copeland."

Pete cleared his throat, stepping closer to draw their attention to him. "Perhaps we could enjoy another impromptu musicale? I've always enjoyed singing."

"An excellent idea." Hank held up a hand, keeping his gaze on Rebecca. "Right after Miss Copeland clarifies what she means by frivolous pursuits."

Pete shook his head in resignation and drew Hope aside, where they were soon speaking animatedly about the kind of crops he and his partner intended to grow in Texas. For all the attention the two of them were paying her and Hank, they might as well have been left alone together.

She squeezed her eyes shut. "Please don't do this, Hank." It was ill-mannered of him to torment her like this.

She heard him step closer. Then his rumbly baritone caressed her ear. "First names again, Rebecca? Or was it a slip of the tongue? Something I suspect doesn't happen very often to a woman like yourself."

"Like myself?" Her eyelids snapped open. "Might I remind you that you know nothing about me?"

"Not true." He smirked at her. "Until a few minutes ago, I was under the mistaken impression you could think of nothing worse than marrying a man like me, but I was wrong."

"Your cockiness is astounding." She struggled to keep her voice light, not wanting to give him the satisfaction of knowing how badly he'd unnerved her.

"Is it?" He spread his calloused hands. "I think we both know you aren't capable of being frivolous. If you were to decide to pursue my hand in marriage, I'm confident you would do it with all earnestness. Likewise, I happen to consider courting a serious business. If I were to pursue you, be assured I would do it with the same level of earnestness. There would be nothing frivolous about it on my behalf or yours."

She blinked at him. Was he genuinely considering following Ms. Monroe's cheeky advice to court her, or was he simply baiting her for the sake of baiting her? It was impossible to tell.

One thing was certain. If he intended to pursue her, it would only be right to confess the truth about her health. Then she would be forced to watch him walk away from her, a prospect that filled her with far more dread than it should have.

Fortunately, Ms. Monroe chose that moment to return to the room. "It's settled," she announced in satisfaction. "The milkman will begin his new deliveries on Monday. And now," she gave Hank a mischievous look, "let us finish haggling the invoice for the transportation of your goods and livestock. If you and Mr. Bishop will meet with me in my office." She gestured imperiously for them to follow her and Rupert.

Chapter 5: Mixed Up Match
Hank

Ms. Monroe's office was bigger than some of the places Hank and Pete had lived in. A large mahogany desk dominated the room. She rolled her wheelchair behind it and fluttered her hands to usher him and Pete into the two Queen Anne chairs in front of her.

"Do take a seat." Resting her clasped hands on her desk, she took her time meeting each of their gazes squarely. "I will confess up front to luring you here under false pretenses. There's no final haggling to be done, since I've decided to write off the balance you owe my company."

Hank frowned in confusion. "We can afford to pay our bills, Ms. Monroe." He had no interest in being treated like a charity case.

"Be that as it may," she looked down her nose at him, not an easy feat from a wheelchair, "I might have need of a well-trained horse from time to time. What better way to get our relationship off on the right foot than by extending the hand of friendship?"

At his silence, she gave a merry cackle. "I've already made my money, Mr. Abernathy. I can afford to be generous. Consider it an early wedding gift."

Pete coughed. "Did you say wedding gift, ma'am?"

She pushed her spectacles higher to get a closer look at him. "You heard me, son."

He tugged at the collar of his shirt, as if needing more air. "As wonderful as that sounds, ma'am, neither of us are betrothed."

Hank had never seen such a tiny woman make his business partner this uncomfortable.

"Your bachelor status won't be difficult to correct," she returned tartly, "though I was a bit put out to discover you'd already met your intended brides. Do not deny it. I could see for myself it wasn't the first time you'd met my lovely guests."

Hank had no reason to deny it. "We traveled from Atlanta to Cedar Falls together, ma'am. It was nothing more than happenstance."

"Was it?" she countered, looking unaccountably pleased by his announcement. "Or maybe it was meant to be. Have you considered that?"

No. Hank was trying to think of Rebecca Copeland as infrequently as possible. It unsettled him to learn that the two southern ladies awaiting their return to the parlor were none other than the "brides" Ms. Monroe had picked out for him and Pete. However, he'd worry about that later. He preferred to deal with money matters first. "We agreed to settle our transport invoice upon arrival, ma'am, and that is what we are here to do."

She waved away his words. "We did, but it's already settled." Her voice was firm, not inviting further protests.

It's not settled in my book. Hank made a point of keeping his accounts square so as not to be in anyone's debt. However, Ms. Monroe's dogged interest in Rebecca and Hope showed no sign of being deterred.

He decided it might be best to let her say her piece. He spread his hands. "What made you decide to match us with Miss Copeland and Miss Thompson?" He and Pete certainly hadn't asked for her interference in their personal lives.

She scowled impatiently at him. "They're a great catch, both of them. Mark my words. If you don't move quickly, they'll be snapped from beneath your noses."

Hank wasn't so sure that Rebecca Copeland's superior attitude was going to make her a hot commodity on the marriage market, but it didn't feel wise to disagree with the railroad tycoon enthroned in front of them. "By moving quickly," he prompted, sensing she would be all too happy to finish the sentence for him.

"Moving quickly means to cease antagonizing your future bride," she sputtered. "I could've cut the tension between you with a knife. It presents a bit of a wrinkle to my plans, albeit not an insurmountable one."

Hank ventured a glance at Pete and found him looking ready to bolt from the room. From the start, he hadn't been a fan of a stranger playing matchmaker in their lives, but Hank was too entertained to tuck tail and run. "There's another wrinkle that very likely *will* prove to be insurmountable, ma'am." She didn't impress him as someone who liked to be wrong, so he was going to especially enjoy poking holes in her plans.

Pete gave the toe of his boot a sideways kick that Ms. Monroe couldn't see. "I think what my business partner is trying to say is that it might be better to let matters of the heart run their natural course."

"Nonsense!" She glared at him. "Young marriageable women are notorious for not knowing their own hearts. They need encouragement. A little nudge now and then from the right people, if you will."

It was plain she considered herself to be one of those right people, which amused Hank all the more. "The wrinkle I spoke of, ma'am, concerns the fact that Miss Copeland has no desire to marry. She was quite outspoken on the point during our journey west." The way she'd recoiled from the idea of being matched with him still stung.

"Neither does her lovely friend." Ms. Monroe's expression plainly indicated she blamed him for that. "She stated it outright to me during the drive here from the train station."

Pete looked so crestfallen by the revelation that another one of Hank's suspicions was confirmed. His business partner was sweet on Hope. "I don't understand," he blurted. "Why would you attempt to match us with ladies who do not wish to be wed? Not that we're asking you to do anything of the sort for us." He shot a pleading look at Hank, begging him to put a stop to this nonsense.

Nodding at him, Hank tried a different tactic, hoping to propel Ms. Monroe into shedding more light on her plans. "I'm inclined to think my friend has the right of it, ma'am. He's never steered me wrong." Other than getting a little sanctimonious at times. Pete could quote a Bible verse for nearly every situation. He was so nice about it, though, it was hard to take offense.

The elderly woman behind the desk gawked at them like they were out of their minds.

A gentle knock sounded on the door, and her expression brightened. "Our tea has arrived."

A maid glided into the room with a silver tray, bearing a porcelain pot steaming from its spout. Three delicate teacups were resting upside down beside it.

Hank felt foolish holding the one she handed him between his thumb and forefinger. It had a gold rim and a riot of dainty bluebells painted on it. He could only hope the tiny handle wouldn't break off in his hand.

Ms. Monroe waited until the maid left the room before returning to her audacious meddling. "I don't believe for a second that Miss Copeland and Miss Thompson are destined to remain unwed. That said," she held up a warning finger, "it'll be up to you to change their minds."

Hank was beginning to wonder if she'd ever had a plan to begin with. Maybe she was simply a busybody who enjoyed butting her head in where it didn't belong. "Then we may be at an impasse." He reached up to finger the scar on his face. "I attempted to court a southern belle once before, ma'am, and it ended up being the biggest mistake of my life. You'll just have to take my word for it."

Ms. Monroe's gaze followed his movements and grew thoughtful. "Is that your biggest objection to wooing Miss Copeland? The fact that she once moved in the highest circles?"

Once? He wrinkled his forehead at her. "Correct me if I'm wrong, but you sound as if you're speaking in the past tense."

"I am." Ms. Monroe leaned his way. "The poor girl lost everything in the war, Mr. Abernathy. Her parents, her brothers, her home, and her fortune. All of it." She slapped her hands on her desk to pound the point home.

It was a shocking revelation, one that didn't ring entirely

true in his ears. He leaned back in his chair and folded his arms. No matter how much Rebecca Copeland had suffered, she most certainly hadn't lost everything. She was very much still in possession of her condescending attitude and uppity ways.

"I'm sorry to hear it, ma'am." Pete's voice was hushed. "Very sorry."

"It's a sad tale, I agree." An unexpected burst of sympathy infused her voice. "Both of them put on a good face for the rest of the world, but what they've endured would've crushed most folks. I dare say their faith is what has gotten them through. That, and sharing the burden together. Goodness knows they don't have much else to their names."

She didn't impress Hank as being a dishonest person, so he scrambled to process her latest claims. It wasn't easy, though. Not with the expensive cut of the gowns both Rebecca and Hope were wearing. No matter how he sliced it, their story didn't add up.

His mind raced over Rebecca's white-faced, pinch-lipped response to the robbery of her reticule. That didn't add up, either. Yes, being robbed was unfortunate, but she'd acted like...

The truth sank home, making him straighten in his chair. She'd acted like every blasted penny she had left to her name was contained in that one small pouch! And if that were true, then it was also possible that the well-tailored gowns the two women still possessed were the last relics from a financial status they no longer enjoyed. *Ach!* As much as he hadn't been looking to give the exasperating Miss Copeland a free pass, Ms. Monroe's explanation certainly put things in a different light.

"What do you know about Miss Thompson?" Pete

pressed during the lull in their conversation. "No doubt she has her own story."

"She's a former slave," Ms. Monroe announced flatly.

Hank's grudge against Rebecca Copeland flamed back to life. "Miss Copeland's slave, I presume?"

"Dear me, no! Her family was very much against the practice of slavery. Her mother was particularly outspoken on the topic, and she practiced what she preached. It wasn't publicly known until after her death that she was vitally active in the Underground Railroad." Her voice grew sad. "A commitment that cut her life short, I'm sorry to say."

What? Hank couldn't believe what he was hearing. One moment, he'd been ready to storm out of the office and stomp past Rebecca Copeland without so much as a backward glance. In the next moment, he was flooded with shame — enough of it to bury him. If everything Winifred Monroe said about the Copelands was true, then he'd sorely misjudged the only surviving member of their family. It wasn't like him to be so unfair, and he could think of only one reason for it. He'd been allowing his past heartache to warp his judgment.

I need to make this right. He wanted to get started today. Right now, in fact. Not because of some half-cocked attempt to start courting the woman he'd been holding in such contempt, but because it was the right thing to do. He couldn't imagine being slammed with so many tragedies at once. As tough as his own childhood had been, he'd been orphaned at an early age — so early that he couldn't remember his parents enough to miss them, and his cruel uncle hadn't been worth missing.

Rebecca Copeland, on the other hand, had a lifetime of memories to sadden her. Shared experiences. Sibling rivalry. Adoring parents who'd undoubtedly rejoiced over her first steps and many other milestones. The thought that he might've unwittingly exacerbated her mourning over her loved ones made his chest ache.

Winifred Monroe's vinegary voice sliced through his thoughts, yanking his attention back to her. "Miss Copeland's mother was very much one of those belles of high society you seem so disenchanted with, Mr. Abernathy." The papery creases at the edge of her mouth tightened. "It was said she could sing like a bird and had a new gown to wear at every party. Acting like a pampered rich woman proved to be the perfect cover for her involvement in the war effort. According to my sources, she single-handedly helped Miss Thompson's family escape north."

"Everyone except Hope, that is," Pete interjected, clearly impatient to hear more about the former slave who'd caught his interest.

"Everyone except Hope," Ms. Monroe agreed. "I don't know why. When the time is right, you should ask her. What I do know is this. The night Miss Copeland's mother lost her life is the same night Miss Thompson's parents escaped."

Silence settled over the office as the two men grappled with the enormity of what she was telling them.

"It's possible Hope stayed behind in Atlanta because she had a sweetheart there," Pete mused in a woeful voice.

Ms. Monroe slowly shook her head. "That wouldn't explain why she traveled across the continent to remain at Miss Copeland's side. The two of them strike me as inseparable."

Hank had gotten the same impression during their train ride, and now he had a better idea why. "Maybe it's because she feels she owes a debt of gratitude to the Copelands," he suggested quietly. "One she's paying back with her undying loyalty." It made sense. It was the only explanation that made sense right now. For someone who normally prided himself on being an excellent judge of character, he'd really blown it when it came to Rebecca Copeland.

Pete looked more distressed than ever. "Miss Copeland appears to be in deep mourning. For all we know, she may have lost more than her family. The war claimed many sweethearts, as well."

Hank's heart sank. He'd been so busy debating why he should or should not court Rebecca Copeland, he hadn't even considered the possibly that her heart was already spoken for. "Maybe that's why she has no interest in marrying."

"That's another bridge you'll cross when the time is right." Ms. Monroe removed her spectacles and set them on her desk. She gave them a warning look. "*Gently* cross that bridge," she stressed. "No galloping into the fray like a bull in a china shop."

Speaking of china reminded Hank of the delicate teacup he was still clutching. He tipped it up and finished drinking his tea before it grew cold.

The moment he set his empty cup on the edge of Ms. Monroe's desk, Pete lightly socked him in the shoulder. "How do you feel about competing with a ghost for a woman's heart?"

"You don't know that to be the case," Ms. Monroe reminded sharply. "This isn't the time to jump to conclusions. It's the time to use every advantage the good Lord has given you to press your suit with these two ladies. You have youth and ambition on your side, hard work and integrity." She gave a girlish titter. "Neither of you are hard on the eyes, either."

Hank snorted at her words, earning him another sharp

look from her. "I know what I look like in the mirror, ma'am." He pointed at his scar. "This face won't be inspiring poetry."

She wrinkled her nose at him. "That's what Keats and Browning are for, Mr. Abernathy. No down-to-earth woman expects her man to spout poetry from sunup to sundown. The main thing she wants is to be loved."

To be loved, eh? It was an odd claim to come from a woman who'd never married, making him wonder about her story all of a sudden. Was her wheelchair the reason for her solitude? Despite her unwed state, her words resonated with him. She was still a woman, so she had the inherent authority to speak from the heart about what women wanted.

"You present a compelling argument, ma'am." He mentally wrote the winning point in her column. Though he'd approached the topic with skepticism, it would be dishonest to continue denying his hopeless attraction to Rebecca Copeland. That was the real burr that had been chafing him lately. No matter how much he'd tried to stop thinking about her, he was unable to. If Ms. Monroe wanted to take credit for the idea, however, he was more than happy to let her. It was easier than confessing the truth — that his feelings had been engaged since the moment he'd laid eyes on Rebecca.

"Then what are you going to do about it?" she demanded.

He shrugged. "I reckon I'll start at the beginning and win her trust."

"You'll have to do more than that." Ms. Monroe made a scoffing sound. "She's not one of your horses, Mr. Abernathy."

"What else would you suggest?" he inquired carefully.

"Everything." She looked shocked at his lack of expertise on the topic. "Wooing a woman comprises everything from small, seemingly insignificant gestures to much grander things like..." She waved her hands animatedly as she searched for the right example to give him.

He steepled his fingers, sensing another verbal sparring match was forthcoming. "Like chasing down a robber to retrieve her stolen reticule, eh?"

"Exactly!" She pointed excitedly at him. Scanning his features, her expression turned to one of astonishment. "Goodness! I assumed you were speaking theoretically."

"I wish." He savored her amazement. "But Miss Copeland was indeed robbed upon her arrival in town."

Ms. Monroe looked fascinated by the story. "And you came to her aid?"

"Pete and I both did." A smug feeling settled in his gut. "She nearly fainted from relief when we returned her reticule to her." He fisted his hands on his knees. "After, of course, we took measures to ensure the fellow would never bother her or Miss Thompson again."

A slow smile stole across Ms. Monroe's lips. "Then I think it's safe to say you've already begun your wooing, Mr. Abernathy."

He grimaced. "I'm not sure she would agree."

"Then change her mind." The spritely old lady impatiently lifted the teapot and motioned for them to bring their cups closer. She refilled them while prattling a mile a minute. "Invite her out to dinner, and sit near her at church on Sundays."

A snicker escaped Pete. "An excellent idea, ma'am!"

Hank sent him a dark look. Pete was well aware his business partner wasn't a church goer. However, the suggestion did have merit.

Ms. Monroe continued talking right over their little side conversation. "You can run errands for the ladies and perform little favors throughout the week. Miss Copeland and Miss Thompson will need to have their classroom set up in the drawing room by Monday morning. There's no telling what all they'll want done between now and then."

Pete abruptly pushed back his chair and stood. "Then there's no time to waste. What do you say, Hank?" He angled his head toward the door, looking anxious to get started on their wooing.

What Hank wanted to say was that his friend was making it sound too easy. Pete had already made significant headway toward winning the friendship of both Rebecca and Hope, whereas Hank had spent most of his time pushing them away.

He huffed out a breath as he stood. "I say we have our work cut out for us if we're going to pursue women who have no wish to be pursued."

"That's the spirit!" Ms. Monroe clapped her hands in approval.

Hank and Pete exchanged a look and burst out laughing.

"I never said it was going to be easy," she protested, looking mildly affronted.

"Oh, you're right about that part, ma'am." Hank sobered. Preparing to head back into the parlor felt like bracing for battle.

"Don't you dare go back into that room without a plan, Mr. Abernathy," she warned.

He gave her the most innocent look he could summon. "Of course, we have a plan!"

"We do?" Pete raised his eyebrows.

"Affirmative. Like Ms. Monroe suggested, we're going to help set up a classroom."

"Now you're talking," Pete returned eagerly. "Let's do it!"

Hank glance over at Ms. Monroe, not wanting to walk out on her without a proper goodbye.

She made a shooing motion at them. "Go! I'll rejoin you shortly." She dipped her head over her desk and started shuffling papers around.

"Yes, ma'am!" Hank shrugged at Pete and exited the room.

As they strode down the hallway together, Pete muttered, "She's right, you know. They're women, not horses."

Hank shot him a curious look. "I am aware."

"Are you?" For a moment, the only sound was the clomp of their boots on the hardwood floor. "Because you were rather cutting to Miss Copeland during the train ride here."

"That's before I knew the truth about her situation." His excuse sounded lame, even to his own ears, but it was all he could come up with at the moment.

"She spread nothing more than goodness and sunshine the entire trip to Texas," his friend pointed out.

It was mostly true. Hank slowed his steps. "Honestly? I couldn't get past the possibility that she'd once owned the woman sitting next to her."

Pete stopped walking a few strides before they reached the parlor. "Is that all?"

"You know it isn't." Hank hated that his friend was forcing him to admit it aloud.

"Good. I just needed to make sure you recognize that Miss Copeland isn't the woman who broke your heart."

Hank glared at him. "Are you done ripping off old scabs?"

Pete glared back. "I would never do that to you."

They faced each other, bristling. "If you start spouting scriptures," Hank gritted out.

"That won't be necessary." The firm set to Pete's jaw didn't invite any more quibbling. "Since you're going to start attending church with me and the ladies we're attempting to court."

"Finally!" Hank wagged a finger at him. "I wondered when you were going to admit to being thoroughly ensnared by a certain brown-eyed beauty."

Pete jutted his chin. "I'm not the one who spent the last week denying it."

It was a good comeback, one Hank couldn't think of a worthy parry for. "Fair enough." He knew when he was boxed in. "But that's not what this is about." He pointed at the parlor. "We're going to march in there and offer to help set up the schoolroom because it's the right thing to do."

"I couldn't agree more." Pete extended a hand to him.

They shook on it. Then they strode into the room together.

Rebecca, who'd been fluttering over the keys of the pianoforte, dropped her hands to her lap. Scanning their features, she lifted her chin. "If you've returned, expecting to be entertained—"

"Not at all," Hank cut in smoothly. "On the contrary, we wish to offer our services for setting up your classroom." Ms. Monroe's home was so big that they shouldn't have any trouble fitting a dozen or so desks in her drawing room, possibly a few more.

Her eyes widened. "You're offering to help us? You?"

The last question she directed in a high-pitched note of disbelief at Hank.

He shrugged, pretending impatience. "Ms. Monroe mentioned you could use some help wiping down and hauling desks from the schoolhouse." He imagined they were covered with soot from the fire. "However, if you already have other help lined up, we'll be on our way." She was accustomed to his aloofness. If he switched tactics too quickly, she might become suspicious.

"Don't mind my partner's prickly manner." As Hank took a step toward the doorway, Pete rounded on the two ladies to declare, "We truly want to help out." If so much hadn't been at stake, Hank would've started clapping noisily to applaud his input.

"One of you does." Rebecca sent Hank a withering look. "But you can't possibly spare the time. Don't you gentlemen have a ranch to run?"

"We do." Hank paused his exodus from the room, half-turning in her direction. "But odds are you'll end up tutoring a future ranch hand or two, maybe even a horse trainer, so it only makes sense for us to contribute." He employed a lazy drawl that was sure to spark a heated response. "But only if you wish. We wouldn't want to be a bother."

A very satisfying haze of confusion swept her features. During the ensuing silence, Hope gushed, "We would be most grateful for your assistance!" She bent to set her teacup on the nearest end table.

"Then count us in." Hank gave Rebecca a triumphant grin just to see her bristle some more.

She stood and gave her skirt an irritated twitch. "I reckon now is as good a time as any to get this over with."

"Agreed," Hank barked before she could change her

mind. "Like you said, we have horses to tend and times a-wasting." Without waiting for her permission, he reached for her hand and tucked it around his arm.

She gasped in outrage as he strolled with her across the parlor toward the front door.

"I'm not sure what you're up to, Mr. Abernathy," she fumed. "You made it quite clear on the train that you can barely tolerate the sight of me. Schoolroom or no school-room, why pretend to be friendly now?"

He couldn't have disagreed with her more, since he was very much enjoying the sight of her flushing and squirming at his side. "Hank," he reminded. "If you can find it in your heart to call me plain ol' Hank, we won't have to keep pretending. We can be friends in earnest."

As they stepped outside together, his chest swelled with pride at the sight awaiting them. Two glossy palominos and a pair of pintos were hitched to his buggy. Despite his humble background, there was nothing humble about the quality of his horses or how well trained they were. They were his and Pete's pride and joy. And there was no way the buggy wasn't up to her standards, with its black leather benches and red-painted wheels. It possessed another very clever accoutrement — a raised bed in the back that could be lowered like a drawbridge to carry a small load.

To his disappointment, she resisted his efforts to lift her into the front seat where he would be driving. "If it's all the same to you, I'd prefer to ride in the back with Hope." She shook his hand off her elbow.

Pete must not have overheard her snippy request, because he was already lifting Hope into the back seat and climbing in beside her.

Hank cocked his head challengingly at Rebecca. "What if I were to assure you that the view is better up front?"

Her face reddened with anger. "You're the most infuriating man I've ever met," she hissed.

"A man with a name that you refuse to use," he shot back, keeping his voice down like she was. "You should try it sometime. It really won't kill you." He held out a hand to her.

"Oh, for pity's sake!" She slapped her hand against his. "Let's not drag this out any longer than necessary. It would be nice to return before nightfall."

Exultation swelled in his chest, making him a little dizzy in the head as he placed his other hand against the small of her back to guide her into the front seat. She was thinner than he'd estimated. The gauzy black shawl looped around her shoulders had been hiding that fact.

Until this very moment, he'd assumed her pale complexion and full rosy lips came from carefully applied powder and paint. However, he had to quickly revise his assessment to something more ominous. It was entirely possible, given the tale Ms. Monroe had just finished sharing, that Rebecca's delicate, fine-boned features were the result of something besides her highborn lineage. Something like hunger.

A blast of righteous indignation made his breathing hitch unevenly. Who had done this to her? The war? A crooked solicitor? Why had her neighbors allowed her to go hungry? Where were her friends?

Rebecca straightened the folds of her gown, giving him an expectant look. "Are you going to gawk the rest of the day, or start driving?"

"Hank." His gaze narrowed on her. "As soon as you say it, we'll be on our way."

"Hank!" She rolled her eyes at him, and declared in a

long-suffering voice, "Hank, Hank, Hank! Are you satisfied now?"

"I'm getting there." His voice came out gruffer than he intended after hearing his name in her haughty southern accent. It sounded so perfect.

And so right.

No way around it, his heart was in trouble where she was concerned. Real trouble.

Chapter 6: Dinner Party
Rebecca

One week later

"It almost feels like we're back in Atlanta." Rebecca flopped wearily down on the bench at the foot of their bed. She was plumb worn out after their first week of teaching school.

"How so?" Hope was humming into the mirror over the washbasin as she straightened her hair and added a lavender bow on one side. She'd fashioned it into the shape of a butterfly. There was no limit, it seemed, to her ability to transform tiny bits and scraps that most women would've thrown away into works of art.

Rebecca counted the reasons off on her fingers. "Number one. She invited Hank and Pete to stay for dinner not once, but twice this week."

Hope raised and lowered her shoulders. "It was the least she could do to thank them for all their assistance in setting up the schoolroom." The two men hadn't stopped at transporting the desks that could be salvaged from the burned-out schoolhouse. They'd also repaired several more and scavenged the town for donations to round out their current collection to an even sixteen desks.

"Number two." Rebecca raised a second finger. "Ms. Monroe's niece, Anna Kate, stopped by for a quick luncheon on our second day of school." She'd brought a tray of dainty sandwiches and a box of petit fours from the bakery downtown that were every bit as sweet and savory as the desserts they'd indulged in back home.

Hope smiled at the memory. "She's lovely, isn't she?" Catching sight of Rebecca's scowl, she quickly added, "Despite the unfortunate fact that she married a northern spy. A former spy," she corrected. One who supposedly could've had the entire Monroe family arrested but chose not to.

Rebecca blew out a breath. "As much as it pains me to relive those days, I think we all can agree he had the moral high ground." Like Anna Kate's husband, the war had placed many fine people in a conflicted position. Her own brothers had been conscripted to fight for a cause they didn't believe in, and they'd paid for it with their lives.

"Thank you for saying that." Hope's dark eyes glistened with too many emotions to name.

Rebecca swallowed hard as she raised a third finger. "Number three. Instead of getting some much-needed rest, our presence has been requested at a full-blown dinner party this evening." Just thinking about it made her yawn. "I'm going to have to drink coffee nonstop to stay awake."

"Oh, surely not!" Hope's eyes snapped with excitement. "We're going to get to meet the lovely Rachel Cassidy and her husband Boone!" They were the owners of the lauded Cedar Falls Finishing School for Young Ladies.

Rebecca chuckled at the bounce of anticipation her friend gave. "Alright. I'll admit I'm looking forward to *that* part of our evening." Their students had been sharing tidbits about the Cassidys all week. The best tidbit was that Boone Cassidy's skin was purportedly as dark as Hope's and Pete's.

"Everyone says Boone is really handsome," Hope sighed dreamily.

"And married," Rebecca pointed out. "Unlike Pete Bishop," she added with a snicker.

Hope gave a twirl that made the ruffled hem of her lavender gown balloon around her ankles. Rebecca had initially lent it to her to travel west in, but she'd refused to take it back upon their arrival. It suited her complexion better than her own. Not to mention Rebecca wasn't sure when she would return to wearing colors. If ever.

Hope gave another twirl and came to a stop in front of Rebecca. "What are you going to wear this evening?"

"This." Rebecca patted the skirt of her black work dress. "All I need to do is wash my face and powder my nose."

Hope looked disappointed. "How long do you plan to stay in mourning, dearest?"

Rebecca stood and moved to the sink. "I'm not sure I'll ever stop." It was something she'd asked herself a thousand times. "My losses are too great. Too heavy." Was it possible to ever be finished grieving for the four family members she'd buried? And what about all the funerals she'd attended for the other young men who hadn't returned from the war? Boys she'd grown up with. Friends. Classmates. Potential suitors. Every last one of their lives had been cut short. It was hardest at night when their familiar faces returned to tug at her heartstrings and chase away her sleep. She didn't deserve to be here anymore than they did — preparing to attend a frivolous dinner party, no less!

She didn't realize she was gripping the edges of the

washbasin until Hope came to stand beside her. "I'll never stop, either," she vowed. "The only reason I didn't wear black—"

"I know." Rebecca plunged her hands into the water and lifted them to her face. Hope didn't have the funds for extras like mourning clothes.

"But if you want me to," Hope offered quietly.

"I don't." Rebecca toweled off her face. "You're the one bright spot in my existence, my friend. I couldn't bear to have the light in you quenched."

Hope gave a sobbing laugh. "To every person who's foolishly asked why I'll never leave you, that is why."

They stepped into each other's arms and hugged each other for a poignant moment.

"What if the Lord has other plans for you?" Rebecca's voice came out muffled against her friend's shoulder.

"He'd have to use a lightning bolt." Hope's slender frame shook with silent laughter. "I'm not sure even that would separate us."

"He could use someone like Pete Bishop." Rebecca raised her head and took a step back, needing Hope to look her in the eye for what she was about to say. "I'll never stand in your way. Never hold you back."

Hope held her gaze. "Pete Bishop is so wonderful that if he asks to court me, I will be inclined to say yes. Even then, I won't give you up. Why can't I have both of you in my life?"

"You will always have me," Rebecca declared fervently. "In whatever place you can fit me, big or small." She was greatly comforted to learn her dearest friend in the world didn't have any plans to replace her.

Hope's expression grew mischievous. "All talk of suitors

aside, I'd rather not make my appearance in the dining room alone."

"Right." It was a gentle reminder that Rebecca needed to finish freshening up with haste.

Hope hovered nearby, helping tuck a few stray strands of hair back into place. Before they turned away from the mirror, she produced another one of her tiny ribbon butterflies, this time in black satin.

"You didn't," Rebecca breathed, watching in fascination as Hope pinned it against the side of her chignon. Though black was a somber color, it stood out dramatically against her white-blonde hair.

"Oh, but I did, dearest!" Hope tucked it in place and stood back to admire her work. "You're the most beautiful woman in mourning I've ever beheld." A twinkle lit her gaze. "I expect I won't be the only dinner guest this evening who thinks so."

"I have no idea what you're talking about." Rebecca was very afraid she did, though.

"Oh?" Hope arched her eyebrows questioningly. "Didn't Ms. Monroe inform us earlier that Hank Abernathy will be in attendance?"

"Did she?" Rebecca pretended to be occupied with smoothing out a wrinkle in her gown. "She's forever popping her head into the drawing room for one reason or another. Sometimes I lose track of her reasons."

Hope snorted. "You wouldn't make a good spy like Anna Kate's husband. I can tell from a mile away when you're lying."

Rebecca lifted her nose. "Only because you've had the advantage of knowing me for so long."

"Or because you're a poor liar," Hope shot back as they

glided toward the door. "The real question is, are you ready to face Hank again?"

"Hank who?" Rebecca teased.

"Yes, indeed." Hope opened the door for her. "You're very bad at lying."

They followed the sound of voices to the dining room. As they paused in the doorway, the three gentlemen present leaped to their feet.

Hank and Pete, who were closest to the doorway, hurriedly pulled out chairs for her and Hope.

The other man in the room was one of the tallest, best dressed black men Rebecca had ever laid eyes on. His shoulders looked broad enough to take on the world. He stepped away from his chair to hold out a hand to them. "I'm Boone Cassidy, and this is my wife, Rachel." He gestured toward the auburn-haired beauty seated to Ms. Monroe's right at the head of the table.

"Pleased to meet you." Rebecca shook his hand warmly. "You, too, ma'am." She experienced a sense of awe as she beheld the highly reputed headmistress of the Cedar Falls Finishing School for Young Ladies. "We've heard so much about your school from our students. Every girl in our class dreams of attending there before they graduate."

Rachel's hazel eyes widened. "Are you serious?"

Her modesty impressed Rebecca. "Indeed, I am. One of our youngest students just this morning claimed that you turn regular girls into royal princesses. Her words, not mine." She could understand the small girl's confusion, since Rachel Cassidy taught things like ballroom dancing and deportment.

Rachel's merry chuckle filled the room. "From what Ms. Monroe has told me about you and Hope, the two of you would fit right in at the boarding school. At the rate our student body is growing, we'll need the additional help soon." Her meaning was unmistakable. She was dangling the proposition of a job offer at them.

Rebecca dazedly took a seat, murmuring her thanks to Hank. "I think I speak for both of us when I say we would be delighted to have that conversation with you." She caught Hope's eye and found her looking equally stunned. "After, of course, our services are no longer needed at the Cedar Falls School." They'd been given no end date, and she had no intention of abandoning the local farm children. In one short week, they'd become too precious to her and Hope.

The headmistress looked ready to run a victory lap around the table. "You heard her. Everyone around this table heard her, which makes all of you my witnesses." She gestured grandly at Rebecca and Hope. "That these two ladies will someday consider helping us transform each and every young lady in this town into a real live princess."

A round of laughter met her words. Even Ms. Monroe's serving staff smiled.

Ms. Monroe interrupted the festivities to say grace over the feast spread out before them. Then everyone began passing the food. There was ham, pot roast, mutton, casseroles, side dishes, and sauces.

There was also the annoying cowboy to Rebecca's right who muttered something designed to singe her ears every time he accepted the next dish she passed his way.

"Thank you, your highness." He had the audacity to wink at her when his large hands settled over the platter of bread and preserves. Whether by mistake or design, his fingers brushed hers during the transfer.

She dazedly spooned some green beans onto her plate before lifting the porcelain bowl to him.

"How kind of you, princess." He kept his voice low enough to torment her ears alone.

She was tempted to whack him with the serving ladle. "Are you going to keep this up all evening?"

He made a big show of glancing around them in astonishment. Then he pressed a hand to his heart and inclined his head at her. "Forgive my momentary loss of speech, your majesty. The honor of hearing you address me directly rendered me speechless."

"A condition you rarely suffer from, I'm sure." Though she wouldn't have admitted it to save her life, her irritation with him was fast fading into amusement. He was shockingly uncouth, but he was the least boring man she'd ever had the privilege of sitting beside at a dinner party.

As Hope had predicted, Rebecca ended up enjoying the evening despite her predisposition not to. Not once did she come close to nodding off to sleep.

Chapter 7: Impossibilities
Rebecca

September

A solid month after Rebecca began teaching school, she could still feel the imprint of Hank's hands lifting her into his buggy during her second evening in town — warm, strong, gentle hands that had left her feeling as weightless as the wild dandelions growing on the side of the road. The memory teased and tormented her, stealing her sleep and making her tired the next day. She constantly grappled with uncertainty, as well. Concerns about what would come next for her and Hope after Miss Carmichael returned to Cedar Falls School — worry about where they would live, what sort of opportunities Rachel Cassidy might or might not offer them at her boarding school, and whether she and Hope would be able to earn enough money to provide for themselves.

This morning was no exception to the constant pressures weighing on her mind. She sat up in bed feeling unsettled and thirsty. Last night, it hadn't cooled off like it normally did. Though she and Hope had slept with the windows open, the dry breeze swirling into the room had been oppressively warm.

Hope was already out of bed, standing in front of the washbasin with a towel in hand. She spun around, wrinkling her nose in concern. "How are you feeling?"

Every shade of horrible. Rebecca forced a smile. "It was a toasty night, wasn't it?"

"That's not what I asked." Hope folded and draped the hand towel on the rung in front of the washbasin. She was already dressed for the day in a new calico gown. Ms. Monroe had given her the fabric, insisting all the unused yardage in her attic would go to waste if her two guests didn't do something with it. Though Hope had ecstatically gone to work making new gowns for both of them, the unexpected gift had added yet another layer to Rebecca's worries. She was far more accustomed to giving than receiving, making her new impoverished lifestyle difficult to adjust to.

"I feel hot, my friend," Rebecca declared in a teasing voice. "Hot enough to drink Ms. Monroe's well dry this morning."

Hope nodded and wordlessly poured her a glass of water. She carried it to the bedside and held it out to her.

"You're too kind." Guilt stabbed Rebecca as she accepted it. "You really shouldn't wait on me hand and foot—"

"Drink," Hope instructed firmly.

Rebecca was too thirsty to argue. She gulped down the water, feeling like she was never going to get enough.

Hope folded her arms and adopted a firm expression. "We need to talk."

Rebecca polished off the glass, chuckling as she lowered it. "We *are* talking."

"I'm serious," Hope insisted. "If you keep this up, you're going to make yourself sick."

Rebecca wasn't sure what she was talking about. "If I could make it cooler, I surely would." It was a lame attempt at a jest.

Hope didn't smile. "I've kept silent, because it's not my place to criticize you or anyone else."

Your place? Rebecca's lips parted in consternation and no small amount of hurt. How could Hope say such a thing? She'd always welcomed her honesty. "You're like a sister to me, so if you have something to get off your chest, by all means." She waved a hand to encourage her to keep talking.

"I do." Hope nodded vehemently. "But I loathe the thought of hurting your feelings."

Rebecca's puzzlement grew. "Have I done something wrong?"

"Not purposely." Hope moved closer to take a seat on the edge of the mattress. "I don't have the right words to say this, but I'll try my best." She clasped her hands so tightly in front of her that the blood left her knuckles. "What ails you is that you're not accustomed to being on the bottom of the pile."

Ouch! A sad chuckle escaped Rebecca. "I think your words are dreadfully accurate. You don't give yourself enough credit." She was constantly reminding everyone around them that she was only present to assist with the classroom and that Rebecca was the "real" teacher.

"Dread." Hope pounced on the word with an aha expression. "That's what I'm talking about. No matter how much help the good Lord sends our way, you don't view it as the gift He intends it to be. Instead, you fear it and dread it, because you're no longer in charge of your destiny." The moment the accusation flew from her lips, her features crumpled in apology. "Oh, dear! That didn't come out at all the way I intended."

"Or maybe it did." Rebecca observed her bleakly. "You're not wrong, my friend. I *am* afraid. Very afraid. More afraid than I've ever been."

"Well, there's no need to be!" Exasperation tinged her friend's voice. "Look around you, dearest." She waved her hands at the lovely suite of rooms they were sharing. "The Lord has provided." Her tone was as matter-of-fact as her unshakable faith. It was something Rebecca had always admired about her.

"But for how long?" The question tore out of her. She knew it sounded ungrateful, but it was exactly the place her faith was in. "The students' regular teacher will eventually return to Cedar Falls, and we'll be at the mercy of our next employer. As nice as Rachel and her husband seemed over dinner, we have no idea what they'll be like to work for. Or what they'll pay us. Or where we'll live next."

Hope shrugged. It wasn't a flippant gesture. She simply didn't have a ready answer. She posed another question instead. "Do you really believe Ms. Monroe will pitch us from her home when that happens?"

Rebecca didn't believe the kindhearted spinster would do anything of the sort, but Ms. Monroe wasn't without her own set of vulnerabilities. "She's bound to a wheelchair, and she's not getting any younger." Rebecca waved at their surroundings like Hope had done. "As comfortable as our current situation is, I can't help being practical. It isn't going to last forever." It might not even last until Miss Carmichael returned to town. Every time Rebecca had tried to bring up the topic with Ms. Monroe, however, she'd stubbornly changed the subject.

"Nothing lasts forever," Hope pointed out in a reasonable voice. She leaned closer to the nightstand to pick up the Bible resting there. Riffling through the pages, she started to read.

Why take ye thought for raiment? Consider the lilies of the field, how they grow; they toil not, neither do they spin:

And yet I say unto you, That even Solomon in all his glory was not arrayed like one of these.

Wherefore, if God so clothe the grass of the field, which today is, and tomorrow is cast into the oven, shall he not much more clothe you, O ye of little faith?

She glanced up from her reading. "Speaking of clothing, I've come up with a marvelous idea for what to do with all that fabric Ms. Monroe has given us."

Rebecca gave a sad chuckle. "I'm sure it's every bit as marvelous as you say it is. You're the most incredible seamstress."

"So are you." Hope looked pleased. "I propose that we sew a new outfit for each of our students. Not only are most of the sweet ragamuffins in sore need of a new outfit, it'll be good advertisement for our other talents." Unlike Rebecca, she hadn't wasted a second worrying about what came next. She'd simply begun preparing for the many unknowns that lay ahead. Her aspirations included opening their own seamstress shop someday.

"All sixteen of them?" Rebecca doubted there was enough light left in the day for cramming that many extra sewing projects into their already full schedule. Their small classroom had grown by three more students in the past week. As word spread about the two temporary teachers, the local farm families had begun to allow more of their children to take a break from the fields and return to school.

At the rate they were growing, they would soon overflow Ms. Monroe's drawing room. Fortunately, the menfolk in town were making steady progress on repairing the damaged schoolhouse. The goal was to return the students there sometime in October.

"All sixteen of them," Hope sang out cheerfully. She dipped her head over the Bible and started reading again. "Can any one of you by worrying add a single hour to your life?"

"You already know the answer to that." With a sigh of resignation, Rebecca scooted her legs over the side of the bed to face another day. Despite the glass of water she'd downed, her knees wobbled beneath her.

Hope stood and reached for her elbow. "Are you sure you feel well enough to teach today? I can handle the students for one morning if you require more rest."

"I know you can." Rebecca didn't want to insinuate otherwise. "But lying around isn't going to make me feel any better." If anything, being left alone would only make the things weighing on her heart feel heavier. Teaching would provide a much-needed distraction. At least until Hank Annoying Abernathy made his next appearance.

She sighed as she reached for the towel by the wash-basin. He'd become the bane of her existence. His frequent, unscheduled visits gnawed at her nerves. She never knew when he would appear or what he would say or do next. One morning last week, he'd hauled in an extra two desks he claimed he'd picked up second-hand. The day after that, he'd crossed paths with the milkman and decided to make the delivery to the Bent Horseshoe Ranch in the man's place.

She reached for her work dress — solid black like the gown she wore on Sunday mornings. Her hand met empty air. She spun toward the hook on the wall, frowning in confusion.

"Were you looking for this?" Hope's voice wafted her way from the other side of the room.

Rebecca frowned at the black dress she was holding up. White rivulets were running down the front of it. She gasped and pointed. "What's that?"

"Bird droppings." Hope's mouth twisted wryly. "One of the risks of sleeping with the windows open, I suppose."

Rebecca's shoulders slumped. There was no time to scrub and dry it before their students began to trickle into the drawing room.

"It's wash day for Ms. Monroe's staff," Hope reminded gently. "As soon as they hear what happened to your dress, they'll insist on adding it to their pile."

Rebecca bit her lower lip, understanding what her friend had left unsaid. Both she and Hope had already sent their church dresses down the hallway to be cleaned. There was only one option left for her — to wear a normal gown, which would officially signal the end of her mourning. It wasn't true, of course. She might never be finished mourning.

Hope wadded up the soiled gown and set it by the door. Moving across the room, she opened the nearest wardrobe and pulled out a fresh gown, one Rebecca had never seen before. "I was saving it for when you were ready," she declared softly, "but I think this morning's events warrant bringing it out sooner."

She moved across the room with a calico gown draped across her arms.

Rebecca caught her breath as Hope paused in front of her. From a distance, the ivory fabric had appeared to be dotted with tiny green leaves and stems. Up close, however, she could see the white magnolia blooms emblazoned across the top of each delicate green stem.

"Oh, Hope!" She reached for the stunning gown. Leaving behind her black dresses suddenly didn't feel as irreverent to those she'd lost. Not when she was replacing it with the magnolias that had once lined her family's property.

She stood in the center of the room, holding the precious gown while tears dripped unashamedly down her cheeks. She was only dimly aware of Hope fetching a hand-kerchief to dry them. And remaining by her side to assist her into the beautiful ensemble. She even helped her button it and tie the sash behind her.

"You're so beautiful, my friend," Hope breathed.

"The gown is, at least. It's a priceless work of art that I'll treasure until the end of my days." Or until she wore it down to its last thread, whichever came first. It was difficult to smile through trembling lips, but she managed. "I can't say the same for the bag of bones wearing it."

Hope threw her hands into the air. "You're doing it again!"

"Doing what?" Rebecca wasn't sure what she'd said wrong this time.

"Giving in to fear." Hope reached up to pinch some color into Rebecca's cheeks for her. "There. That's better." With one last worried look at her, she opened their bedroom door and waved her into the hallway ahead of her.

They grabbed a quick bite to eat in the breakfast room, then made their way into the drawing room. A cluster of children were squatted down on the floor playing jacks.

One of the girls leaped to her feet at the sight of her and Hope, waving her arm wildly in the air. "Miss Copeland! Miss Thompson!"

Rebecca hurried forward. "Is everything alright, Cassie?" She eyed the threadbare dress the eight-year-old was wearing. It barely came to her dusty knees, underscoring just how right Hope was about the wardrobes of their students.

"Yes'm." The girl lowered her arm, ducking her head in embarrassment. "It's just that I..." She flushed. "Need to, er, make a trip to the powder room. Please, ma'am."

"By all means, love." Rebecca shooed her toward the door in the back of the room.

The child spun away in a flurry of faded fabric and bare feet.

Hope moved to her side, murmuring in a low voice. "We can get started this evening on a new dress for her."

"With a pinafore." Rebecca was fully convinced of the merits of the plan. "And a pretty bow beneath her chin." If she had it her way, they would doll up each and every girl like the princess Cassie dreamed of becoming.

"Of course." Hope's voice was cautious. "Not too fancy, though. We don't want extra fripperies that'll get caught on fences, trees, or farm equipment."

Her thoughtfulness was touching. "You think of everything," Rebecca sighed.

Hope made a wry sound. "Only because I've had my skirt and sleeves snagged on just about everything."

More students arrived, including two scuffling boys. One of them was holding a bleeding nose. It took several minutes to sort out what had happened. They got the first boy's nose cleaned up and the second boy assigned to clean the privy before the end of the day. Rebecca had quickly learned to apply the capricious energy of her students to chores. Not only did it discourage infractions, it helped keep the premises in good repair for everyone else.

She and Hope herded the students to their desks and began a new day of learning with a prayer and the Pledge of Allegiance. No sooner did they get everyone seated than the room erupted into pandemonium.

"Mr. Hank," the children squealed.

"Mr. Hank!" Cassie clapped with so much enthusiasm that she nearly fell out of her chair.

"It's Mr. Hank, Miss Copeland," another boy called to her, as if she hadn't heard all the other times the dratted man's name had been bellowed.

It appeared everyone in town was on a first name basis with Hank Abernathy, including her students.

"Now what?" Her insides fluttered with a thousand misgivings as she turned around to clash gazes with her nemesis.

Hank's tall frame and broad shoulders filled the entrance of the drawing room. Despite the amount of time he spent training horses, he always looked combed and scrubbed down when he visited the schoolroom. The amount of trouble he went to in order to impress her benefactor was puzzling. She'd yet to figure out what hold Winifred Monroe had over him.

"I hope I'm not interrupting anything," he drawled, not looking the least bit apologetic. He knew he was interrupting her classroom. It was something he did again and again and again. If anything, he looked pleased with himself.

She should've been angry with him. She had every right to be, but her traitorous heart lurched over the happy grin plastered across his face.

The scolding she should've given the children over the noise they were making never came as they erupted from their seats to launch themselves like cannonballs at their guest. It was a game they played every time he showed up.

He held his arms straight out from his sides while they tried to figure out how many could latch on to him like little monkeys. This time, four of the smallest children managed to hang off of one arm while three slightly taller children swung from his other arm.

He had no trouble lifting all seven of them off the ground to their giggling delight. Rebecca tried to ignore the flutter in her heart from watching his display of strength. The cocky cowboy was showing off, of course. She'd witnessed him do it so many times by now, it shouldn't still have this effect on her.

But it did.

Warmth and wonder melted her insides every time she watched him carrying on like an oversized boy with her students. It was endearing how much he adored spending time with them. Though she would never admit it to him, it was something they had in common. Granted, his methods were far louder and more disruptive than hers, but she couldn't deny the light in his eyes as he pretended to groan and complain from the effort of lifting the squirming children. His antics made them dissolve into giggles, lose their grip, and slide one-by-one to the floor.

Hank didn't stop there, though. He always hung around a few extra minutes to tug on ponytails and wrestle with the boys.

Rebecca waited until he neared the end of his routine before gliding across the room and planting herself directly in front of him. She folded her arms and pinned him with her most ferocious scowl. "To what do we owe the pleasure of your visit this time, Mr. Abernathy?" She tapped the toe of her boot impatiently.

"Watermelons, ma'am." He gave her a crooked grin that made her heart melt a few more degrees. So did the way his gaze ran appreciatively over the new gown she'd all but forgotten she was wearing.

Her students dissolved into another round of cheering at his unexpected reply. "Watermelons, ma'am," they repeated, attempting to mimic his much deeper voice.

She shook her head at him, tamping down on the urge to laugh. He didn't need any encouragement. He was mischievous enough without it. "Explain yourself, sir."

"That's what I've been trying to do since the day we met." He reached out to playfully tap the end of her nose. "I like your new dress, by the way."

She froze beneath his touch. He'd done it so naturally and so affectionately that it robbed her of her breath. The fact that the children were witnesses to her utter lapse of decorum didn't do one thing to restore her equilibrium.

He held her gaze for a breathless moment before continuing, "I have a whole wagon full of watermelons that need to be eaten before they go bad. Claim as many as you want for you and your students. I'll find someone else to take the rest of them off my hands."

She lost her battle with her composure and smiled. Oh, how she loved watermelons! How had the dratted man figured it out? Then again, she might be giving him too much credit. Maybe he'd been simply calculating how to create the biggest ruckus among the youngsters surrounding them. Regardless of his motivation, she was grateful for the watermelons. It was all she could do not to throw her arms around him to thank him with a hug.

The students formed a circle around the two of them, joining hands and chanting, "Watermelons, watermelons, watermelons!"

Rebecca glanced around the room for Hope's assistance, but she'd mysteriously disappeared.

Ms. Monroe rolled into the room with a look of astonishment. "What's the meaning of this?" She peered admonishingly at them over her reading spectacles, but the lines around her mouth relaxed when she perceived who was at the root of the commotion. "Hello, Hank! What brings you to the Bent Horseshoe Ranch this morning?"

"Watermelons," Rebecca supplied without dropping Hank's laughing gaze. "This loco rancher brought us an entire wagon load of them."

"Indeed?" Ms. Monroe sounded delighted. "If all this yammering is any proof, I'd say the children will be happy to indulge in them *at lunch time*." She pointed at the clock on the wall, eliciting a round of groans. "Does it look like lunch time to you? No? Then let's get back to our school work. The time will go faster if our minds and hands are busy."

Rebecca waved the crestfallen students back to their seats. "You heard her, my dears. It's time for all of us to get back to work. Shh, boys! Girls!" She raised a finger to her lips to admonish the more talkative ones. "Aaron and Jason, you have math to practice. Get out your slates." She kept a warning eye on them until they complied. "I'll be over to check your progress in a few minutes."

Ms. Monroe watched the room settle back into orderliness with a look of pride. She nodded at Rebecca who nodded back. It had been more than generous of her to lend the use of her home to the school children. She possessed a heart of true charity. It was no wonder the whole town looked up to her, including the mayor.

"Hank?" Ms. Monroe beckoned him to come with her. "If I could have a word with you in my office?" She smiled reassuringly at Rebecca. "Don't worry. Your watermelon delivery man isn't in any trouble. We just have a bit of business to discuss."

My watermelon delivery man? Rebecca liked the sound of that more than she should have. So much so that her cheeks grew warm.

A wave of lightheadedness shook her as she returned to her desk. Once Ms. Monroe and Hank were out of sight, she propped her elbows on the desktop and dropped her forehead against her clenched fists. *What is wrong with me?* Maybe Hope was right. Maybe she'd been wallowing so much in her worries about the future that it was making her sick.

Or maybe the cause of her sudden weakness was something else entirely. Like the way Hank Abernathy made her feel. She'd been serious about her plans to grow into an old spinster. She was never supposed to get so attached to the maddening man with all of his maddening ways. She wasn't supposed to be thinking about him as often as she breathed air, forever wondering when his next visit would be.

I'm such a fool. At some point during the past month, she'd gone from despising the man to caring for him. Deeply. For the life of her, she didn't know what to do about it. It went against everything she'd planned for her future. The possibility that he might be interested in her in return didn't make her feel any better. He deserved better than a woman with a weak body that would almost certainly lead to a childless marriage. He'd proven beyond the shadow of any doubt that he loved children as much as she did. She couldn't do that to him. She wouldn't!

"Rebecca?" A man's voice anxiously interrupted her reverie. "Are you alright?"

It was Hank. The one person in the world she had no business thinking about but couldn't ever seem to push from her mind. She would simply have to find a way to do so.

She lifted her head, hating the wave of dizziness brought on by such a simple gesture. "I'm fine. Thank you," she snapped. "I was just saying a prayer. You should try it sometime."

"You sound like my business partner." His upper lip curled at her. "Always preaching and spouting scriptures."

She caught her lower lip between her teeth. "In my experience, the Bible only offends those who are in the wrong."

Anger glinted in his eyes. "You sure don't mince words."

She hated treating him like this, but it would be better for both of them in the long run. "Will you allow me to pay you for the watermelons?" She was too weary to engage in another bickering match.

His jaw tightened. "I think you know the answer to that." He pivoted away from her. Then he lurched back in her direction. "On second thought, there *is* something you could do to repay me."

"Oh?" Her heartbeat quickened at the determined look in his eyes.

"Ms. Monroe informed me she's hosting a charity ball in a few weeks. It's the annual fundraiser for the Widows and Orphans Christmas Fund."

Ms. Monroe was hosting the fundraiser? It was news to her. "Such a worthy event!" She'd heard about the ball, but she honestly hadn't expected to receive an invitation. The monetary contribution of a school teacher wouldn't make a drop in the bucket toward a cause like that.

Hank removed his Stetson, running a hand through his

wind-tossed hair, mussing it further. "If you save me a dance, it would square us up for the watermelons."

"I, er...wasn't planning on attending." She shook her head helplessly at him. "Are you certain it's taking place at the Bent Horseshoe Ranch?"

He gave her a rigid nod.

"Very well." She knew without waiting to be told that Ms. Monroe would insist on her and Hope's attendance. "One dance."

"Thank you." He loped from the room before she could say anything else, clapping his hat on his head as he stepped into the foyer.

Rebecca stared after him, openmouthed, wondering what had just happened. Her thoughts were in a tangle the rest of the school day, making it difficult for her to concentrate on the needs of her students. She even misspelled a simple word on the chalkboard, which Hope was quick to correct. Discreetly, of course.

By the time she retired to their bedroom, she was an emotional wreck. She shut the door quietly behind her and slumped face down on the bed. During the heartbreaking years of war, she'd taught herself how to cry silently. They all had. Otherwise, no one at her home in Atlanta — family members or hired staff — would've ever gotten another full night's sleep. The tragedies had come upon their household so quickly and so viciously that she'd been unable to recover from one funeral before she was planning the next one.

Rebecca had buried her mother, father, and two brothers in the space of a single year. And now she was in the complicated position of pushing away the only man she'd ever cared for this way. Knowing she was doing the right thing didn't make it any easier.

I love him.

It was the truth. *I love him so much that it hurts.* Though it didn't change anything, it was a relief to finally acknowledge it, at least to herself. She wept over the way he adored the farm children, certain he would make a doting father someday. She wept over his callused hands and scarred face that had become inexplicably precious to her. She even wept over his pithy comebacks to her many attempts at putting him in his place. He'd proven he could take her southern sass and dish it right back. If she'd been in the market for a husband, he would've been her perfect match.

But she wasn't.

The only choice she had left was to hide her feelings from him. Forever. He deserved to marry a woman whose body was whole, a woman who could bear the children he longed for, a woman strong enough to reign as the mistress of his home.

If only she'd stayed home the summer she'd turned fifteen, instead of accepting what she thought was a marvelously grown-up invitation to visit a distant cousin in Florida. Her parents had encouraged the visit, because they thought it would get her farther from the battle lines drawn between the north and south, which it had. What it hadn't protected her from was the outbreak of scarlet fever that had swept her cousin's town.

She'd returned to Atlanta a much frailer version of herself, never to return to her normal weight and strength. According to her doctor, the fever had additionally rendered her body unable to bear children. The Copeland legacy would die with her.

"There you are, dearest!" Hope's voice permeated her

abject misery, though she was still too emotionally wrung
out to roll over and face her friend.

She pushed herself weakly to her elbows. "Just give me
a minute to compose myself."

Hope's footfalls flew in her direction. Strong, capable
hands reached for her. "Rebecca, honey, what's wrong?"
She rolled Rebecca over and gave a startled cry. Gathering
her close, she pressed her ravaged face against her shoulder.
Hope's fingers frantically probed for injuries and brushed
across Rebecca's forehead to check for a fever.

"I love him," Rebecca choked. "I love him so much."

Hope continued her poking and probing. "I'll inform Ms.
Monroe how poorly you're doing. She'll call for a doctor."

Rebecca doggedly continued her confession. "I just
today realized what was happening to me. I've been so
blind. So very blind!"

"That's the fever talking." Hope made a clucking sound
as she unbuttoned Rebecca's collar and fanned her face.
"You'll feel better after we cool you down." She gently laid
her back on the pillows. Then she hurried to the washbasin
to dampen a cloth. Returning to Rebecca's side, she used it
to bathe her forehead.

"Don't you see?" Rebecca struggled to sit up, but Hope
held her down. "This lovely house, all the beautiful things
in it, the music, the schoolroom, the happy children, the pile
of watermelons Hank delivered today..."

"I'm well aware of how many watermelons that loco
cowboy delivered," Hope retorted. "I'm the one who helped
Pete carry them to the kitchen. There were thirty-two of
them, dearest. Thirty-two! We have watermelons coming
out of our ears!"

"He's a mess, isn't he?" Rebecca was half laughing and

half weeping by now. "With all of his impromptu visits and gifts and the way I foolishly look forward to every one of them. I enjoy our time together, Hope. I even enjoy our bickering. I crave it as much as my next breath, which is why I have to leave Cedar Falls."

"What?" Hope gave her an admonishing scowl. "I've never heard you talk out of your head like this before. It's time to fetch the doctor. I'll be back as soon as I can with something to drink. Just..." She stood and held her hands up, palms facing out. "Stay there."

"Did you hear me?" Rebecca gave a violent shiver. "I'm leaving Cedar Falls."

"No, you're not." Hope's voice grew hoarse with emotion. "We're finally getting settled, and it's starting to feel like home."

"Not to me." Rebecca swung her head from side to side in agitation. "I can't do this anymore, Hope. I'm not asking you to leave with me. I wouldn't dream of taking you away from Pete or that lovely shop you'll undoubtedly open someday."

"Rebecca!" Hope sounded agonized.

But Rebecca wasn't finished. "Please forget the let's-be-spinsters-together nonsense. You'd be a fool to let Pete Bishop slip through your fingers. He has eyes for you and you alone."

"Enough!" Hope clapped loudly, making Rebecca's ears ring. Her eyes flashed brown fire. "I'm not the only one with a man whose heart belongs solidly to her." She held up a finger to halt Rebecca's spluttering. "It's my turn to talk and your turn to listen." She bent over the bed to push back a strand of damp hair from Rebecca's face. "Your ranting only confirms what I already suspected, dearest. What *everyone* already suspected. Why half the town already has your name paired with his!"

Rebecca grew limp as the fight oozed out of her. "They can't," she moaned. "We can't. You know why."

Hope said something that she couldn't understand, and the walls of the room blurred. Then everything faded.

Chapter 8: New Plans
Hank

Two days later

Hank felt like he was living in a nightmare he couldn't wake up from. He went through the motions of getting out of bed, tossing on his work clothes, and heading to the barn; but his thoughts remained on one thing only.

One woman.

Rebecca had to get well. She just *had* to, because his life would no longer be worth living if she didn't. He couldn't bear the thought of not having any more bickering sessions with her, or getting to watch her pretend to be irritated with him every time he showed up unannounced to her classroom. He especially loved the way her whole face lit with adoration for the children she and Hope got to teach. She loved children so much that her insistence on living as a spinster made less and less sense with each passing day. He'd been living in the hope of changing her mind someday. At the moment, however, he simply wanted her to live to see another day.

Rebecca had been thrashing in bed with a fever for forty-eight hours straight. Ms. Monroe had promised to send word the moment she turned the corner. Unfortunately, he'd yet to receive word of that hoped-for news.

He whistled to get Red Sabbath's attention. In response, his stallion eagerly thrust his head over the stall door. "Come on, boy!" He opened the stall. "You're going to help me run an errand."

Pete leaned out of the adjoining stall with a pitchfork in hand. "It's about time you showed up." From the amount of hay clinging to his clothing, it looked like he'd been up working for a while.

"I apologize for my tardiness and for leaving you alone this morning. I'll make it up to you, brother." Hank was grateful to have such a hardworking business partner. Unfortunately, he was going to have to rely on his hard work more heavily today than he would've preferred.

"We have a set of ranch hands to help out." They'd hired a second one only days earlier, which didn't keep Pete's dark features from creasing with worry. "I presume you're heading to Ms. Monroe's place?"

Hank shook his head. "If I thought my presence would do a lick of good, I would. I think my time will be better spent at the church."

"Oh?" Pete's eyebrows flew upward.

Hank grimaced at him. "You're welcome to save your gloating for after I leave to have a long overdue talk with our Maker." His voice cracked.

Pete tossed aside his pitchfork and gave a whoop of exultation.

"I said *after* I leave," Hank reminded dryly as he saddled his horse.

Pete broke into a celebratory jig, swinging his Stetson in

a circle over his head. One look at his partner, however, had his steps slowing. "I'm not making light of Rebecca's condition, but we've committed her to the Lord's hands, and there's no better place for her to be."

"*You've* committed her to the Lord's hands." Hank's mouth twisted bitterly. "I've never had an honest conversation with Him. I've spent too much of my life being angry about all the bad things He allows to happen." He yanked his hat brim lower. "But if I'm going to be asking the Lord favors, it only seems fair to get to know the One I'm talking to."

Pete nodded soberly. "It's all I've ever wanted for you, brother."

Without any further ado, Hank swung himself into the saddle and lifted the reins. "Let's go, Red Sabbath!" He dug in his heels.

The moment they exited the barn he nudged the stallion into a gallop. His hooves pounded against the hard-packed earth, kicking up dust. They flew past farms and livestock, creek beds and clusters of cedars until the small white church building drew into view.

Hank slowed Red Sabbath to a canter and then to a walk to give him time to cool down as they approached the building.

A man in a straw hat and overalls was tying a horse to the hitching post when Hank arrived at the front door.

"Howdy!" The man straightened and shaded his eyes to take a cautious look at Hank. "I don't believe we've met."

Hank leaped to the ground. "I'm Hank Abernathy, one of the owners of A & B Ranch."

The man's expression brightened. "I've already met your business partner and happen to think the world of him." He strode over to Hank with a hand outstretched.

"I'm Pastor Nathan Daniel." His brown hair waved over his ears, extending into a pair of sideburns.

"It's good to meet you, sir." Hank shook his hand.

"You don't need to call me sir. Pastor Nathan will do."

Hank liked his humble attitude. "Pete won't stop singing your praises. When I left the barn earlier, he was dancing a jig over the thought of me darkening a church door."

Pastor Nathan sobered. "It's harder for some folks than others, but God is patient." He helped Hank tether his horse and added a few buckets of water to the trough on the other side of the hitching post.

"I don't think I'm the sort of fellow the Lord will want to be bothered with," Hank said cautiously, "but I'm not here for me. I'm here for somebody else." His voice broke. "I can only hope I've come in time."

Pastor Nathan ushered him through the front door. They stood together in the vestibule, absorbing the quietness inside the building. "If this was a social call, I'd invite you to my office. However, I sense your visit pertains to a more serious nature."

Hank turned impulsively his way. "The woman I love is ill. She may be dying."

"Ah." Pastor Nathan nodded gravely. "Come with me." He led Hank down the center aisle of the sanctuary. The rustic wooden pews gleamed with polish, and an enormous cross filled the back wall of the platform in front of them.

The minister gestured reverently at it. "Would you like for me to pray with you, or would you like some time alone with Him?"

"Alone, I think. Thank you, pastor." Hank appreciated the fellow's low-pressure approach.

"If you have any questions, I'll be right on the other side

of that door." Pastor Nathan pointed to a door to the right of the platform.

Hank waited until he was alone in the room before dropping to his knees at the altar. "If You're real, I could really use Your help right now." When it had come to the things he'd endured while growing up, shaking his fist at the sky had given him a modicum of satisfaction, but Rebecca deserved better than that. She needed *him* to be better than that.

At first the conversation felt one-sided as he expressed his disappointment about all the things that had gone wrong in his life. "But then You sent Pete my way, Lord, and I started seeing things differently." The way Pete approached life was nothing short of profound. He trusted God with everything. Every goal. Every plan. Every decision. In the past, Hank had tried to write off the way he clung to his faith as weakness, but Pete wasn't weak. Pete was one of the strongest men he knew, body and soul.

"I was wrong about You, Lord." That was the sticking point. "The truth has been staring me in the face for years." In the form of Pete Bishop, his dearest friend in the world, a man who was closer to him than a brother.

Something lightened in his chest as he finished making his peace with the One who'd hung on a cross similar to the one hanging in front of him. Then Hank started praying in earnest for the woman who held his heart in her hands.

Rebecca Copeland might not want his heart. Upon reflection, he didn't blame her. He hadn't lived a perfect life. He'd been hardhearted and cranky. Though he'd been trying to make up for it ever since their disastrous first encounter, he didn't feel like he'd made much headway, and no wonder. He wasn't the sort of fellow most women would dream of having for a husband. Regardless, his heart belonged to her, like it or not, and he was fairly certain she didn't like it.

That no longer mattered, though. His heart's cry was no longer to impress her. It was to see her get well and get out of bed once again.

"Heal her, God. I'm begging you. The students need her. Cedar Falls needs her." *I need her.* He spoke the final sentence inside his head, since this wasn't about him. "Make her whole."

In that moment, Hank would've done anything to hear her voice again, to be scolded one more time by her. He would've volunteered to trade his life for hers, if it were possible. She was a beautiful person, inside and out. She deserved to live.

The door to the church opened and closed behind him. Soft footsteps approached him. Then the sound of a woman weeping filled his ears.

He opened his eyes to see who was kneeling beside him, and his chest grew cold.

Hope's face was ravaged with grief and she gazed at the cross in front of them. Tears spilled down her swollen cheeks, leaving salt stains on the front of her dress.

For a moment, Hank couldn't breathe. "Is she—?" He choked out the words, unable to complete the sentence.

"She's a f-fighter, Hank. Th-that's all I can tell you." Hope sobbed out the words.

His shoulders slumped at her confirmation that Rebecca was still alive.

It took her a moment to collect her emotions enough to speak again. "She beat a fever before, but this is different. To be frank, I'm not convinced she ever fully recovered from the last one." She drew a shuddery breath. "It was during the war. Her parents sent her to Florida to visit a cousin, thinking it would get her further away from the fighting. They had no way of knowing they were sending her into an outbreak of scarlet fever."

Hank's blood chilled all over again. "Scarlet fever, you say?" From what he understood about the illness, it left many of its victims with devastating, lasting effects.

Hope nodded brokenly. "That's why she refuses to marry. She may never be able to have..." She broke off the rest of what she was about to say, ducking her face shame-facedly. "I had no right to say that. It's not my story to tell."

Hank sat riveted as he finished what she'd started to say inside his head. *She may never be able to have children.* So many things about Rebecca Copeland grew abruptly clearer. Her undeniable love for children, coupled with the way she constantly blew hot and cold with him. Maybe that was the reason she was forever pushing him away. Maybe he'd been wrong in assuming she objected to him. If anything, she probably thought she was protecting him from herself!

He staggered to his feet, reeling from Hope's inadvertent revelation. "I need to see her." He needed to see her today. Now!

Hope shook her head, making more tears break loose. "The doctor isn't allowing visitors. Not even me. He fears we'll contract whatever illness has her in its jaws."

"I don't care," he growled. "They'll just have to make an exception." He stomped up the aisle of the church, leaving Hope kneeling at the altar in open-mouthed shock.

The ride to Ms. Monroe's ranch didn't take long. He left Red Sabbath in Rupert's capable hands. The fellow came across as stuffy and devoid of emotion. However, he served his mistress as loyally as a soldier in the presence of a commanding officer. It was good enough for Hank.

One of the maid's let him into the house with a polite curtsey. The moment he stated his business, however, her expression grew bleak. "No one is allowed in the sick room, sir. It's too risky."

He watched her gaze sidle down the main hallway, telling him that Rebecca's room was on the first level. Moments later, a man wearing a bird mask backed slowly from one of the rooms, pinpointing exactly which door led to the bedside of the woman he loved.

His heart pounded at the realization that the man approaching them must be the doctor. Though he'd never been around anyone deathly ill before, he'd heard about the horrific masks and helmets that many physicians wore to protect themselves from disease.

Poor Rebecca! If she was slipping in and out of delirium, she might easily mistake the fellow for a monster.

The man removed his mask as he reached the foyer. "Let madam know there's been no change in our patient's condition."

"Yes, sir." The maid curtseyed to him, looking sad.

As the physician departed the house, an idea struck Hank. "May I speak with Ms. Monroe?"

The maid looked uncertain. "I don't know if she's taking visitors, sir, but I'll find out. Who's asking?"

"Hank Abernathy from A & B Ranch."

She nodded and spun away from him. The moment she disappeared from view he tiptoed down the hallway and paused outside Rebecca's door. He had no idea what condition he would find her in on the other side. All he knew was that he had to find out.

He'd prayed, and God had heard his prayer. He was certain of it. And if God chose to answer his prayer, then there was nothing to fear.

Unsure when the maid would return, Hank twisted the handle and pushed open the door. Then he stepped inside and noiselessly shut it behind him.

The first thing that became apparent to him was that the room smelled stagnate and stale. The second thing that became apparent was the outline of the woman in bed was motionless.

Fear momentarily gripped him, but he pushed through it. *I prayed for God to make her whole, and He heard me.* If big, strapping Pete could believe in stuff like miracles, then so could Hank.

He wrinkled his nose at the dank scent in the room, wondering whose idea it had been to deprive the woman he loved of fresh air. Making his way to the windows, he pushed them open one-by-one. A wholesome breeze wafted into the room, making it instantly easier for him to breathe.

"Hank?" A faint voice wafted his way.

He spun around in astonishment. "Rebecca?" His feet started moving in her direction.

She stirred in bed, blinking in puzzlement at him. "Where are we?" Her voice sounded slurred. "What's going on?"

Relief flooded him so strongly that he was forced to take a knee beside her bed. "You've been ill." His voice was husky with emotion. "But you're well now. I prayed for you. Everyone who cares for you has been praying."

She struggled to sit up, raising the covers to her chin. He lent her a hand, hating how fragile her fingers felt. "That's the cockiest thing you've said to me yet, Hank Abernathy."

He stared blankly at her. "For praying for you?"

She gave him a withering look. "No. For claiming I got well because *you* prayed for me."

He snorted. "Pardon me, Miss Copeland, but isn't that

how prayer is supposed to work?" He was tickled to no end to hear her crabbing at him. It was enough to make his eyes grow damp.

She smoothed her hands over the blanket. "It strikes me as a little high-handed for anyone to take credit for it."

He grinned through the sheen of dampness covering his eyes. "Pete's forever telling me God listens to sinners' prayers. Now I know for myself that it's true."

Her expression softened. "Did you really pray for me, you heathen?" Her normally tidy hair was mussed, but she'd never looked more beautiful to him.

"I did." Throwing all caution to the wind, he reached for her hands again. "I couldn't stand the thought of you no longer being here to scald my backside over watermelons and such."

Color flooded her face as she stared at their joined hands. "You're as ornery as the lads in my class, always up to mischief."

He couldn't deny it. "Maybe I need someone in my life capable of taking me in hand and softening my rough edges."

She shook her head at him, looking distraught. "I can't be that for you, Hank. I'm sorry, but I just...can't." She tried to pull her hands away from his, but he held on to them.

"Because of your first fever, eh?"

Her lips parted on a mortified gasp. "Who told you?"

"It doesn't matter." He clenched his jaw. "Because I prayed for you, and you got well. I didn't know what ailed you, so I prayed for all of you, you hear? I begged God to make you whole. Those were my exact words."

"You really are that cocky, aren't you?" She shook her head at him, looking like she wasn't sure if she should burst into tears or laughter.

"Confident is the word I would prefer." He didn't care how loco it sounded to her or anyone else. "If there's anything to this faith stuff, then that's how it should work. I don't intend to spend the rest of my life serving some mealy-mouthed God who isn't capable of doing squat."

She burst out laughing, but it ended on a sob. "You've never hesitated to say what's on your mind. I should've known you'd be just as frank with the Lord." She pointed upward with tears spilling down her cheeks.

He decided that now was as good a time as any to press his suit. "I want to marry you, Rebecca, but it's not because of the number of children you may or may not give me. I want to marry my favorite sharp-tongued southern belle, because she's you. Only you."

Her lips parted in wonder. "Hank!"

"Rebecca!" He tenderly twined their fingers together.

"But you've never even told me you love me!" A delicious shade of pink infused her face, chasing away her pallor.

"Then I'll tell you now." He gazed deeply into her eyes. "I love you, Rebecca Copeland, whether you like it or not."

A shaky chuckle eased from her. "I like it, Hank."

"We can build something solid on that, sweetheart." He believed it with everything in him. "Someday you might even love me back." A fellow could dream, anyway.

"Not someday," she corrected softly. "As much as I deplore admitting it to someone with as big a head as yours, it's already happened."

He gave a whoop of happiness that made her wince. The sound was probably loud enough to raise the roof another inch or two.

Voices babbled in the hallway. Doors opened and slammed closed.

Perceiving they would soon have company, he leaned closer to her, bringing their lips a mere inch apart. "After the scare you gave me, I think it's fair to say you now owe me two dances at the charity ball."

"Deal," she agreed softly. "I might even make it three dances for good measure."

Chapter 9: Charity Ball
Hank

November

For reasons Hank didn't understand, Rebecca had sworn him to secrecy about the new understanding between them. He wasn't clear if she'd even told Hope about their confessions of love to each other. For now, though, he was content to no longer be her arch enemy.

He continued to interrupt her classroom as often as he wanted to. Not only was it impossible for him to go very long without seeing her, he thoroughly enjoyed every second he got to spend with the students.

Occasionally, he caught her watching him with a pensive look and wished he knew what she was thinking. It was bad enough knowing that something was troubling her. It was even worse wondering if she was having second thoughts about the direction their relationship was heading.

Though he'd declared his interest in marrying her, he hadn't outright asked her to do so. It was a matter he intended to rectify soon. He was just waiting for the perfect moment. In the meantime, he made every second in her presence count. He brought her fresh eggs and produce straight from his gardens. He built her a new chalkboard. He asked her opinion on everything, from wallpaper designs to what he should name his newest batch of horses.

The evening of the charity ball arrived. He and Pete donned their Sunday best suits. Pete's was slate colored. Hank's was black. Since he owned only one suit, it made sense to ensure it was appropriate for church, funerals, and any other dress-up occasions. To make it look less funereal, he paired it with a white dress shirt and a silver bolo, hoping he wasn't breaking any rules by keeping his boots and Stetson on.

Fortunately, Pete kept his boots and hat on as well, ensuring there'd be at least two cowboys present this evening.

"Did you ask Rebecca to the ball?" Pete ducked his head in the mirror, catching Hank's eye as he straightened his bolo.

"I asked her to save a dance for me, and she said she would." Technically, she'd offered to save him three, but he couldn't think of a way of telling Pete without breaking his promise to her.

"One whole dance, eh?" Pete straightened and tipped his hat at a jaunty angle. "You sure know how to go overboard with the ladies, Romeo."

Hank ignored his jibe. "She promised to save one for you, too."

Pete's wide mouth twisted into a self-satisfied smirk. "Hope might allow it if it's only one dance. She's feistier than she appears once you get to know her." He adjusted his hat to a different angle. "Very possessive, too, when she's courting a fellow." He didn't sound the least bit displeased about that last item.

Hank had never seen him this happy, and he didn't begrudge him one bit. No one deserved to be happy more than Pete. "Love looks good on you, my friend."

Pete gave him a sly look. "It doesn't look too shabby on you, either."

"If you say so." Rebecca was a complicated woman with a complicated past. He didn't want to rush her into anything she wasn't ready for. Her secret would be safe with him for as long as she wanted.

"I just did." Pete waggled his dark eyebrows suggestively at him, inviting him to say more.

Hank pretended not to notice as he patted his pocket to ensure the wad of money he never traveled without was intact. Never again would he be the poor, helpless urchin who'd arrived barefoot on a ship to a new and foreign country. He was a man of means now. "I know what I'm doing with her, Pete. You're just going to have to trust me."

Pete's grin disappeared. "I followed you into battle, didn't I?"

Hank wished he could think of a way to give Pete a hint about what was really going on between him and Rebecca — something she wouldn't consider a breach of trust now or in the future.

However, Pete started speaking again before Hank could make up his mind how much or how little to say about his secret courtship. "I plan to ask Hope to marry me. Maybe as soon as tonight." He withdrew a small silk bag from the pocket of his trousers. Pulling open the drawstring, he dumped the contents of the bag into the palm of his hand. A marquis diamond glinted up at them.

Instead of saying anything, Hank withdrew the black velvet box he'd slipped into his pocket after getting dressed. He lifted the lid to reveal a gold band shaped like the curved branch of a magnolia tree. A trio of magnolia blooms were soldered to it. In the center of each magnolia, a round diamond blazed. The diamond in the center was the biggest.

"I sent off for a custom-made ring," he shared quietly. "I wasn't sure they would be able to do what I was asking."

Pete's gaze glittered with approval. "It's perfect for the lady in question."

"The ring you picked out is just as perfect for your real-life princess," Hank assured. "Assuming they say yes to what we're about to ask them. They've been inseparable for so long."

"It's yet another reason we'll make the perfect husbands for them." Pete couldn't have sounded more certain. "You and I are business partners, and they'll be living within a stone's throw of each other at A & B Ranch."

"What if it's not enough for them?" Hank didn't feel like he was betraying any secrets by sharing his deepest fears with his closest friend. "Sure, I can offer her a nice home to live in and plenty of money to spend, but she's already had those things. Her parents gave her everything money could buy. She was raised in a mansion and adored by everyone, with two brothers to protect her honor. She's educated, accomplished, and well traveled." He shook his head. "How I can possibly measure up to all of that?"

"All she really needs," Pete countered, "is your love. You're a man she can trust. Someone who will make her feel safe again." He grimaced. "Hope has indicated to me on more than one occasion that Rebecca hasn't had a decent night's sleep since she lost everything. According to Hope, she's been fretting herself to a thread over what will happen to them after Miss Carmichael returns to town to reclaim her post."

"Lord willing, *this* will happen." Hank shook the black velvet box in the air at him.

It was the perfect solution to the next set of challenges Rebecca and Hope would soon be facing. If only he and Pete could convince them of it!

REBECCA STOOD IN FRONT OF THE LONG DRESSING mirror in their bedroom, smoothing her hands down the sides of her empire waist gown. "You really outdid yourself this time, Hope."

"Thank you, dearest. I'm glad you approve." Hope had been inundated with custom orders for tonight's ball. Word was quickly spreading around Cedar Falls about her extraordinary talent as a seamstress. The orders were pouring in. Rebecca helped as much as she could. She wasn't a shabby seamstress herself, but Hope was the real genius behind their designs. At the rate they were gaining new customers, it wouldn't be long before they could afford to open their own shop.

Rebecca tried to tell herself it would be enough to reach the point where they wouldn't have to worry about money any more. Lately, however, she'd found herself longing for more — things a person couldn't put a price tag on. Things like love, marriage, and children. Though Hank had professed his feelings for her, he hadn't followed it up with an actual marriage proposal. Maybe she'd thrown off his plans by insisting they keep their courting a secret for a while. In her defense, however, she'd experienced a miracle only minutes before they'd declared their love to each other. She'd been famished and slightly dehydrated at the time. She hadn't been thinking straight.

But now she was, and she was filled with angst over why Hank hadn't pressed her harder to become his affianced. Was he having second thoughts about marrying a woman who might not be able to bear children? It was terribly sweet for him to believe his prayers had completely healed her, but it was a leap of faith she hadn't been able to take with him yet.

"It's time," Hope announced, coming to stand beside her in front of the dressing mirror.

They were wearing matching gowns. The only difference was that Rebecca's was a pale pink, and Hope's was a crisp blue — the color of icicles clinging to the eaves of a home in the wintertime. Both gowns boasted a gauzy layer that hugged the skirt and trailed on the floor behind them. They would need to pin it up before they started dancing. Hope had hidden a special clasp in the folds of the fabric for this purpose.

"Are you nervous?" Rebecca's heart was racing like a runaway train.

"A little," Hope admitted, "but in a good way."

Rebecca couldn't say the same since she wasn't as confident in Hank's ultimate intentions toward her as Hope was in Pete's intentions.

They glided up the hallway together only seconds before their favorite horse trainers made their appearance. The two men entered the two-story entry foyer and paused beneath the elegant chandelier to greet Mayor Reggie North. A stringed quartet was playing a familiar holiday tune in the great room around the corner where the ball was just getting started.

A pair of cedar trees towered on either side of the foyer. They were trimmed with ribbons, berries, and hand-carved trinkets. Since tonight's event was designed to raise money for the Widows and Orphans Christmas Fund, Ms. Monroe had spared no expense in decorating her home for the holidays. Garlands draped the stairwell bannisters and doorways, and the scent of fresh-baked pastries and pies filled the air.

Rebecca slowed her steps, drinking in the sight of Hank in his church clothes on a non-church day. The fact that he and Pete still had on their hats and boots was especially endearing.

Once a cowboy, always a cowboy. She liked the fact that they weren't attempting to be something they weren't. During her initial launch as a debutante into high society, she'd been a little too quick to judge a man by his family name and the size of his bank accounts. How far her tastes had evolved since then! Nowadays, she cared more about the faith, integrity, and work ethic of a prospective suitor than any of those other things.

Mama and Daddy would've been proud of who I've become. It was a comforting thought. Rebecca had lived to see their biggest dreams come true in a country where all people could now live in freedom. Oh, how she wished they could've seen this day for themselves!

She had one additional dream she wished they could see. One more dream that hadn't yet come to pass. One she was trying her hardest to entrust to the Lord instead of taking things into her own hands.

All in God's timing, as Hope was so fond of saying.

Hank's head finally turned in her direction, and all other thoughts ceased. The world stopped spinning and time stood still as their gazes met and held. The look he gave her spoke volumes that transcended the crowded, noisy gathering. He was as glad to see her as she was to see him. No words were necessary. She just knew.

He wove his way determinedly around the other guests to stand in front of her. "I believe you promised me a dance, Miss Copeland?"

Her heart fluttered nervously, but she was unable to resist the temptation to tease him back. "Are you that ready to collect your dues and make your escape, Mr. Abernathy?" Shortly after they'd met, they'd fallen into a habit of sniping at each other. It was something she'd come to enjoy more than she cared to admit.

He gave her a mock sardonic look as he crooked an arm at her. "You're so much in my debt, Miss Copeland, that a hasty escape won't be possible. According to our last tally, you owe me no less than three dances, though I suspect you're still shorting me."

Rebecca slapped her hand down on his arm, reveling in how solid it felt beneath her fingers. Unless she was mistaken, he flexed it for her benefit. She rolled her eyes at Hope, who had her hands wrapped demurely around Pete's arm. "If this scoundrel monopolizes my time for too long, do send a rescue party." With her spare hand, she swiftly buttoned up her train to avoid tripping herself or anyone else with it.

Hope's delighted trill of laughter followed them as Hank twirled Rebecca into the great room. The dance floor was already filled with twirling couples.

He looked down his nose at her. "I don't know why I continue to trifle with such a cruel, cruel woman." More cedar trees lined the outer edges of the room, draped with gold ribbons and endless strings of red berries.

Her breathing grew shallow as he caught her against him. "Maybe it's because you know deep down that you instigate most of our arguments."

"Guilty as charged, ma'am." The music transitioned to a

slower, sweeter piece that allowed them to sway from side to side for a bit. He held her gently, like he was afraid she might break. There was a vulnerable light in his eyes as he gazed down at her. "When you became ill, my biggest fear was that you would never be able to verbally box my ears again. It was an unbearable thought."

She felt like she was drowning in the adoration radiating from him. "I wouldn't have to keep my boxing gloves on if you weren't constantly saying and doing things to get a rise out of me."

He drew her close enough to defy the bounds of propriety. "It's because nothing in this world gives me more joy."

For a breathless moment, she was certain he was about to kiss her, but the dance ended.

A sharp ringing sound drew their attention to a platform erected on one side of the fireplace. Someone had lifted Ms. Monroe and her wheelchair to the center of it. She was holding up an enormous bell and tapping it with a metal wand.

The stately Rupert was stationed at her side in a black suit with an intricately folded tie circling the neck of his wintery dress shirt. He had his hands raised to buy the silence of the crowd gathered in front of them.

The moment the voices in the room muted to a dull murmur, he gestured grandly for Ms. Monroe to speak.

"Welcome, all of you!" She graciously fluttered her heavily be-ringed hands at them. "Thank you for attending our annual fundraiser for such a worthy cause. We'll begin with a few announcements designed to lighten your hearts as well as your pocketbooks."

A round of laughter worked its way through the room.

Her sparkling gaze roved the audience and landed on Rebecca. "Many of you have been privileged to meet the two delightful young ladies who traveled hundreds of miles to fill the teaching vacancy in our schoolhouse. For those of you who haven't yet made their acquaintance, I'd like Miss Rebecca Copeland and Miss Hope Thompson to join me on the platform."

Rebecca caught her lower lip between her teeth and melted against Hank's side. "She could have warned us," she hissed to him.

His low baritone rumbled in her ear. "Just picture me interrupting your class and forcing you to glove up, princess." He gave her a gentle nudge to get her moving toward the front of the room.

Hope met her at the base of the platform, looking as abashed as Rebecca felt over being drawn into the spotlight. They stepped onto the platform with their arms locked tightly together.

"We've faced worse things," Hope whispered as they faced Ms. Monroe, who promptly waved at them to turn around and face their audience.

Hope's words didn't have their usual comforting effect. Rebecca found herself anxiously seeking out Hank's gaze. Only when she latched on to it did the butterflies in her stomach settle to a more manageable swarm.

She was dimly aware of Ms. Monroe singing her and Hope's praises from behind them. She was too busy imagining the floor opening up and swallowing her and Hope whole. "While Miss Copeland and Miss Thompson are present this evening to rally behind the widows and orphans in this town, what most of you may not know is that Miss Copeland is an orphan herself."

What? Her words made Rebecca jolt in alarm. She gripped Hope's arm harder, wondering what in tarnation

Ms. Monroe was up to this time. She didn't desire the woman's sympathy or anyone else's.

She could barely breathe while she listened to her kind benefactor give a brief but glowing address to commemorate Rebecca's late mother's contribution to the war effort. And her tremendous sacrifice. Ms. Monroe went on to describe her and Hope's contributions to the citizens of Cedar Falls, to include the dozens of hours they'd spent sewing new clothing for every student in their care.

"Much-needed and much-appreciated gifts to our precious farm families!" Ms. Monroe blew a few kisses to Rebecca and Hope, eliciting a smattering of clapping and cheers from her listeners.

The acceptance Rebecca felt in the room made tears of gratitude burn behind her eyelids. She blinked rapidly to hold them back, but they trickled from the corners of her eyes and streaked down the sides of her face. So much for the powder she'd applied before leaving their bedroom!

"For this reason," Ms. Monroe concluded, "it is my greatest honor and privilege to make the first donation this evening toward the seamstress shop these two hardworking teachers have been saving for. My donation will include an engraved plaque in Mrs. Clara Copeland's honor for them to hang in their shop."

As the room dissolved into noisy cheers of approval, Rebecca and Hope threw their arms around each other to absorb the wonder of what was happening. Then they rushed to Ms. Monroe's side to enclose her in a tearful embrace.

"I love you like the daughters I never had." Ms. Monroe's voice crackled with emotion as she pressed kisses to their cheeks. "You've brought so much joy to my home. So much life. So much music. So much love."

Rebecca was so dizzy with happiness that she missed a step as she exited the platform. She would've gone tumbling to Kingdom Come, but Hank was there to catch her.

Rebecca clutched his shoulders to regain her footing. "Let me guess," she accused shakily. "You're going to use this as an excuse to wrangle another dance out of me."

"Guilty again." He led her through the crowd to an area of the room that was less crowded. "At the rate things are going, I'll be stuck here the rest of the evening." They were stopped countless times by folks Rebecca had never met to receive well wishes about her and Hope's future seamstress shop.

While she and Hank were chatting and making new friends, Ms. Monroe tapped her bell again. This time, it was to announce the return of the town's beloved schoolteacher, Miss Charlotte Carmichael.

The breath caught in Rebecca's throat as her gaze latched on to the woman she'd been half-hoping she would never have to meet. She was a homespun looking creature with her salt-and-pepper hair pulled back in a bun and a plaid shawl draped around her plump shoulders.

The cheer of celebration that arose rivaled the one the citizens of Cedar Falls had given her and Hope. It was clear that Miss Carmichael was dearly loved, a sentiment she'd earned through years of selfless service. It was something Rebecca couldn't find in her heart to begrudge, no matter what the woman's return meant for the two teachers who'd temporarily filled her shoes.

She'd known from the moment she and Hope accepted their positions that this day would come. Why, oh, why did it have to come so soon, though? A month before Christmas, no less? When everything in their lives was finally settling into some modicum of normalcy?

Rebecca's Dream

She sought out Hope and found her clinging to Pete's arm as tightly as Rebecca was clinging to Hank's arm. They drew shuddery breaths as they silently acknowledged they would soon be stepping into the next set of unknowns. Due to the tall, ruggedly handsome cowboys at their sides, however, it was a less scary prospect than it had been upon their arrival in town.

But unknowns were still unknowns. They would be full of twists and turns, both good and bad. They would be corners a person couldn't see around. Mountains they would have to trust God to help them climb. No longer being in charge was something Rebecca wasn't sure she would ever completely adjust to, though she was making slow and steady progress.

A blur of movement caught her eye as the crowd parted to make room for Rachel Cassidy's tall, dark, former bounty hunter of a husband. Boone made his way to them, shaking a warning finger at her and Hope. "My wife sent me through the throng to remind you of your promise to interview for positions at the Cedar Falls Finishing School for Young Ladies. She says we can work out a teaching schedule that will allow you to simultaneously juggle the demands of your seamstress shop. She even mentioned the possibility of incorporating your shop into the school itself. My sister, who isn't a shabby seamstress herself, helps out where she can; but it's too much for one person." He spread his hands. "As you can imagine, a bevy of young princesses in the making requires an endless number of ball gowns, party dresses, riding habits, ribbons, and lace."

An *oh* of delirious wonder escaped Hope. She launched herself at Rebecca, and they exchanged another jubilant hug. Rebecca sought out Boone over the top of her friend's shoulder. "Yes! Please tell Rachel we said yes!"

He nodded in satisfaction. "We'll be in contact to set up your interviews and work out the particulars." As he backed away from them, the bell chimed again.

This time, it was held high in Pete Bishop's hands. It took some time for the noise in the room to dim enough for him to be heard. "My business partner and I would like to make the next donation to the Widows and Orphans Christmas Fund on behalf of A & B Ranch. We also have one more very special announcement to make. It's more of a request. Or rather, a pair of requests." He handed the bell back to Ms. Monroe and leaped off the platform to stride back to where Rebecca and Hope were standing.

He made a beeline toward Hope and took a knee in front of her. Then he reached in his pocket to remove something that he held up to her. It was a diamond ring that glinted beneath the glow of the chandeliers, eliciting gasps of astonishment from those standing nearby.

It took an extra moment for Rebecca to realize that he and Hope weren't the only reason for the gasps.

The weight of her hand on Hank's arm shifted as he took a knee in front of her. The squeals and murmurs of the onlookers might've made it hard for them to overhear what he said next, but she heard it.

Every word of it. All the way to the deepest parts of her soul.

"Will you marry me, Rebecca?" His heart was in his eyes as he added, "No one else is even capable of filling the role of Mrs. Hank Abernathy."

A half dozen pithy rejoinders bubbled to her lips, but her heart was too full to squeeze out more than one word. "Yes!"

Hope said yes a split second later, and the two cowboys

leaped to their feet to slide the engagement rings on their fingers.

The magnolias and diamonds sparkled up at Rebecca with the promise of new beginnings. Then Hank's arms came around her, cuddling her closer so he could mutter in her ear. "Fair warning, darling. This means you're officially stuck with me until the end of your days."

She rose to her tiptoes to touch her lips to his, leaving him and everyone around them with no doubt about her feelings on the topic.

Epilogue
Rebecca

One year later

The kick made Rebecca catch her breath. She reached for her blooming belly, silently begging for another kick. Feeling the life growing inside her never grew old. The impossible had happened to her and Hank. The miraculous kind of impossible.

A few months into their marriage, they had conceived! She was still a handful of weeks from her delivery date, but she doubted she would last much longer. She already felt and looked big enough to burst.

The second kick was much lower, and the third one was nowhere near the other two. Maybe the baby was kicking and punching at the same time. She wouldn't put anything past the offspring of Hank Abernathy.

Casting an anxious look at the clock on the mantle, she noted the time. It would be another hour before Hank returned from the horse ring where he and Pete were training their newest batch of foals.

The horse breeding business at A & B Ranch was

booming. They had orders coming from all over the Midwest, straight up through the heartland, and back down to the southernmost borders of Texas. As it turned out, folks were willing to get on a waiting list and pay extra for Hank's and Pete's horses. It wasn't just because of the growing popularity of Missouri Fox Trotters in the area. Ranchers were attesting right and left that the horses Hank and Pete personally trained were smoother to ride and better at herding cattle. Rebecca couldn't have been more proud of her husband and his highly skilled business partner.

A knock sounded on the front door.

"Come in," she called.

Hope's dark, beautiful face appeared. "There you are, dearest!" They never failed to share a daily visit. Lately, though, Hope had been making the walk between their farmhouses more often, insisting that Rebecca needed her rest.

"Where else would this mother duck be waddling off to?" Though Rebecca tried to make light of her condition, she'd woken up this morning feeling truly miserable. "Oh, Hope! I can barely eat, sleep, or even breathe these days. I'm beyond ready for Baby Abernathy to make his or her appearance."

"And they will. Soon, dearest." Hope's belly was starting to swell, too. She and Pete had announced a few weeks earlier that they, too, were in the family way.

"They?" Rebecca frowned, wondering if her friend had misspoken.

Hope didn't answer. She merely reached out to place a hand on Rebecca's belly and was promptly kicked. "Ouch!" Her voice was teasing. "Manners, Little Abernathy!"

Rebecca sighed. "He's been active all afternoon. It's like

having a whole litter of kittens squirming and scrapping inside of me."

Hope adopted a faraway look, reaching for Rebecca's belly again. "May I examine you? As you are already aware, I did a little midwife training back in the day."

It wasn't something they spoke of often since Hope's training was a throwback to her time of servitude, but Rebecca trusted her skills implicitly. "Examine away, my friend." She couldn't tell by Hope's expression if there was any cause for worry or if her friend was simply being her usual attentive, caring self.

At Hope's commands, Rebecca turned this way and that, even lying down on her side on the sofa so Hope's efficient hands could palpate her belly more thoroughly. A heavy sigh escaped her friend. "I think I know why the baby feels like it's grown an extra pair of elbows and knees."

It was a fitting description for all the kicking and punching Rebecca had endured lately. She yawned and struggled clumsily to sit up. "Do tell!"

Hope lent her a hand to finish tugging her upright. "You're expecting twins, dearest."

"Twins!" Rebecca shrieked out the word, glancing frantically toward the barnyard where Hank was still working.

THAT NIGHT, SHE LAY IN HER HUSBAND'S ARMS, murmuring the word again and again. "Twins. We're having twins. How in the world is that possible?" She knew she was keeping him awake, but she couldn't stop marveling over the double miracle they'd been handed. As far as she knew, there were no twins in the Copeland family tree. This would be a first for her family.

He grinned in the moonlight pouring through their windows. "I have a few ideas how it might've happened, darling." He pushed up on an elbow to deliver a tender kiss to her.

"Delivering on your promise to torment me until the end of my days," she sighed against his lips. "You did warn me. I'll give you that."

His grin turned wicked. "I was actually going to say it's because of how much I love you." He rolled to his back and tucked his hands behind his head. "It only makes sense our kind of love would produce two babies instead of one." He couldn't have sounded more proud of that fact. Or more smug.

Her laughter rang out, filling the night with all the anticipation she couldn't contain. "I married a very cocky rancher."

"I'm only stating facts." He reached for her hand to lace their fingers together. "I understand who's ultimately responsible for every miracle we've been given, Mrs. Abernathy."

"I do, too." Waves of contentedness washed over her. This was the side of Hank Abernathy that the rest of the world didn't get to see. A man who strove every day to deepen his relationship with his Maker. A man who was fiercely loyal to everyone he loved. A man who gave more than he took. A man who'd lasso the moon itself to ensure her happiness. A man she would never tire of sitting across the table from. The one and only man she wanted to grow old with.

Her sense of warmth and contentedness grew stronger and spread. It was followed by a sharp pain in her midsection.

"Hank!"

He shot straight up in bed. "Yes, darling?"

"I think it's time." Her voice shook.

"Now?" He sounded winded.

"Yes, now. I know it's early, but..." She moaned as another cramp gripped her. "I need Hope. Please, Hank! I need her right now."

He rolled out of bed, snatched his hat from the bedpost, and sprinted for the door.

Rebecca had survived war and tragedy, but she couldn't recall ever being more afraid than she was in the minutes Hank was away. This was happening too soon! She stared helplessly at the walls and ceiling as wave after wave of pain crashed over her.

She longed to leave the room and return when it was all over, but that wasn't an option. There was no way around the suffocating wall of pain. No shortcuts. No detours. The only way through it was forward.

"You've brought us this far, Lord," she begged. "Please don't abandon us now." Her body was a living, breathing miracle. The babies on their way were gifts from Heaven. She knew all of this, yet her faith wavered. "I'm so scared," she gasped into the empty room.

"There is no reason to be, dearest." The door flew open, and Hope sailed into the room. "Just breathe, my friend. In and out. In and out, the way we practiced."

Rebecca did as she was instructed, gulping back sobs of relief. Now that Hope was in the room, her confidence was restored over the odds that everything would be alright.

Hank was on her heels, and Pete was with him. Hope barked orders like a general to the two of them, calling for a basin of warm water and clean towels. "Lots of them," she stressed. "Pete, how about you fetch the doctor? It's early in her labor so we should have plenty of time, but it's twins we're talking about. I don't want to take any chances."

He gave his wife a look as tender as a kiss before taking off to saddle his horse.

The next few hours passed in a blur of radiating pain for Rebecca. It was punctuated by the grip of Hank's hand on hers and the sound of Hope's calm and steady voice. The doctor arrived and added his encouragement to the mix.

Just when Rebecca feared she might not have the energy to push a single time more, a baby's cry filled the room.

All she could do was weep with relief. *One down, one to go!*

"Our son is perfect, darling. Thank you." Hank's voice was hoarse with emotion. "All ten fingers and all ten toes."

"Peter Lincoln Abernathy," Rebecca panted. It was one of the many names they'd picked out, but it seemed the most fitting at the moment. Their first son would be named after Hank's closest friend and Rebecca's father. "I know it's a mouthful, but we can call him Linc for short." *Just like Daddy.*

Their daughter arrived next with a piercing cry that drowned out the wails of her brother. "Clara Hope Abernathy." Rebecca's face was drenched with tears, but they were happy ones. It meant the world to her to be able to name her daughter after her mother and the woman who was closer than a sister.

"Thank you, dearest!" Hope bent to examine her patient once again and exchanged a few hurried whispers with the doctor. "Another one?" Her voice rose incredulously. "Rebecca, honey! There's a third baby on its way!"

Rebecca laughed through her tears, summoning every

ounce of strength she had remaining. "I'm running out of names, Hank. Think hard!"

He rocked little Linc in his arms, gazing down at her with a face as damp as hers. "It depends on whether you're giving me another son or another daughter, Mrs. Abernathy," he drawled.

Within minutes, a second son made his appearance. They promptly named him Jonathan Michael Abernathy after her two brothers.

Hope bathed and swaddled the three babies. Then she tucked them in Rebecca's and Hank's eager arms, all but collapsing in her husband's embrace afterward.

"Ms. Monroe is sending an army of servants to help out, dearest," she assured with a yawn. "We'll stay until they arrive."

THE NEXT FEW WEEKS WERE FILLED WITH BABY WAILS, night feedings, exhaustion, and love; but Rebecca and Hank tackled the new challenges together. In an unexpected show of charity, the widows at the Ladies' Church Auxiliary set up a schedule for volunteers, eagerly taking turns to help out with everything from cooking to cleaning to changing diapers at A & B Ranch.

Their assistance allowed Rebecca to steal a few minutes alone here and there with her husband. They didn't venture far, usually settling for a turn on the porch swing where they could gaze at the stars together.

Tonight was one of those evenings. Hank tipped her chin up to deliver a tender kiss. "I didn't know it was possible to be this happy."

"Nor did I." She kissed him back. "Or to have one of my biggest dreams come true — three times over!" Getting to spend the rest of her life loving him was her biggest dream come true.

"My pleasure, Mrs. Abernathy." He drew a finger down her cheek.

"There you go, taking all the credit like you're so good at doing." She rolled her eyes at him, but that didn't keep her from leaning in for another kiss from the cockiest cowboy in the west.

"I would do it again." Hank raised his head, smoothing the tendrils of hair back that the breeze kept blowing across her eyes. "The long ship journey here, all the years of indentured servitude, every time I went to bed cold and hungry. I would do it again and again and again to be with you." He kissed her like he was never going to stop. "And our precious family." He ran his thumb across her lower lip. "And the life we've built together."

She kissed his thumb. "I love you for saying that. I love you for being you." She wrinkled her nose mischievously at him. "No matter how many times you wear down my last nerve."

He winked at her. "I'm God's gift to your nerves, Mrs. Abernathy."

The stars twinkled, and the moon shone overhead, illuminating the joy and laughter they read in each other's eyes.

Thank you for reading
Rebecca's Dream.

Jo Grafford, writing as Jovie Grace

A woman living under an assumed name fights her attraction to the federal marshal tracking her outlaw brother in
Lawfully Ours.

Sneak Preview: Lawfully Ours

L*ove and the law collide in this sweetly suspenseful historical romance.*

U.S. Marshal Jack Holiday is on a special mission to track down and apprehend a notorious cattle rustler from his Robin Hood-style crime spree. More legend than man, Billy Bob Flint steals from the rich to fatten the barnyards of the poor.

Unbeknownst to the rest of the world, the rogue's sister is living under the assumed name of Cat Southerland, while serving as the beloved seamstress of Cedar Falls. When Jack rides into town, brandishing an arrest warrant for her brother, she realizes the new life she's built for herself may soon come crumbling down around her ears. Torn between old loyalties and her unexpected attraction to the tough but honest federal marshal, Cat struggles to keep her ties to Billy Bob a secret.

Jo Grafford, writing as Jovie Grace

Grab your copy of
Lawfully Ours
today!

Keep turning for a peek at the spinoff series!

About Jovie

Jovie Grace is an Amazon bestselling author of sweet historical romance filled with cozy suspense and swoony cowboys. She also writes sweet contemporary romantic thrillers as Jo Grafford. To join her New Release Email List, visit www.JoGrafford.com.

For the most up-to-date printable list of her sweet historical books:
Click here
or go to:
https://www.jograffford.com/joviegracebooks

For the most up-to-date printable list of her sweet contemporary books:
Click here
or go to:
https://www.JoGrafford.com/books

Happy reading!

Jovie